THE TRAIL OF THE SWORD,
Complete

By
Gilbert Parker

First published in 1894

Published by Left of Brain Books

Copyright © 2023 Left of Brain Books

ISBN 978-1-396-32426-0

First Edition

PUBLISHER'S PREFACE

About the Book

Trail of the Sword is a novel by Sir Gilbert Parker.

About the Author

"Sir Horatio Gilbert George Parker, 1st Baronet PC (November 23, 1862 - September 6, 1932), known as Gilbert Parker, Canadian novelist and British politician, was born at Camden East, Addington, Ontario, the son of Captain J. Parker, R.A.

He was educated at Ottawa and at University of Trinity College. Parker started as a teacher at the Ontario School for the deaf and dumb (in Belleville, Ontario). From there he went on to lecture at Trinity College. In 1886 he went to Australia, and became for a while associate editor of the Sydney Morning Herald. He also traveled extensively in the Pacific, Europe, Asia, Egypt, the South Sea Islands and subsequently in northern Canada. In the early nineties he began to make a growing reputation in London as a writer of romantic fiction."

(Quote from wikipedia.org)

CONTENTS

DEDICATION

My Dear Father:

ONCE, many years ago, in a kind of despair, you were impelled to say that I would "never be anything but a rascally lawyer." This, it may be, sat upon your conscience, for later you turned me gravely towards Paley and the Thirty-nine Articles; and yet I know that in your deepest soldier's heart, you really pictured me, how unavailingly, in scarlet and pipe-clay, and with sabre, like yourself in youth and manhood. In all I disappointed you, for I never had a brief or a parish, and it was another son of yours who carried on your military hopes. But as some faint apology--I almost dare hope some recompense for what must have seemed wilfulness, I send you now this story of a British soldier and his "dear maid," which has for its background the old city of Quebec, whose high ramparts you walked first sixty years ago; and for setting, the beginning of those valiant fightings, which, as I have heard you say, "through God's providence and James Wolfe, gave England her best possession."

You will, I feel sure, quarrel with the fashion of my campaigns, and be troubled by my anachronisms; but I beg you to remember that long ago you gave my young mind much distress when you told that wonderful story, how you, one man, "surrounded" a dozen enemies, and drove them prisoners to headquarters. "Surrounded" may have been mere lack of precision, but it serves my turn now, as you see. You once were--and I am precise here--a gallant swordsman: there are legends yet of your doings with a crack Dublin bully. Well, in the last chapter of this tale you shall find a duel which will perhaps recall those early days of this century, when your blood was hot and your hand ready. You would be distrustful of the details of this scene, did I not tell you that, though the voice is Jacob's the hand is another's. Swordsmen are not so many now in the army or out of it, that, among them, Mr. Walter Herrim Pollock's name will have escaped you: so, if you quarrel, let it be with Esau; though, having good reason to be grateful to him, that would cause me sorrow.

My dear father, you are nearing the time-post of ninety years, with great health and cheerfulness; it is my hope you may top the arch of your good and honourable life with a century key-stone.

Believe me, sir,
Your affectionate son,
GILBERT PARKER.

15th September, 1894,
7 Park Place,
St. James's S.W.

INTRODUCTION

THIS book, like Mrs. Falchion, was published in two volumes in January. That was in 1894. It appeared first serially in the Illustrated London News, for which paper, in effect, it was written, and it also appeared in a series of newspapers in the United States during the year 1893. This was a time when the historical novel was having its vogue. Mr. Stanley Weyman, Sir Arthur Conan Doyle, and a good many others were following the fashion, and many of the plays at the time were also historical-- so-called. I did not write The Trail of the Sword because it was in keeping with the spirit of the moment. Fashion has never in the least influenced my writing or my literary purposes. Whatever may be thought of my books, they represent nothing except my own bent of mind, my own wilful expression of myself, and the setting forth of that which seized my imagination.

I wrote The Trail of the Sword because the early history of the struggles between the French and English and the North American Continent interested me deeply and fascinated my imagination. Also, I had a most intense desire to write of the Frenchman of the early days of the old regime; and I have no idea why it was so, because I have no French blood in my veins nor any trace of French influence in my family. There is, however, the Celtic strain, the Irish blood, immediate of the tang, as it were, and no doubt a sympathy between the Celtic and the Gallic strain is very near, and has a tendency to become very dear. It has always been a difficulty for me to do anything except show the more favourable side of French character and life.

I am afraid that both in The Trail of the Sword, which was the forerunner of The Seats of the Mighty, the well sunk, in a sense, out of which the latter was drawn, I gave my Frenchman the advantage over his English rival. In The Trail of the Sword, the gallant French adventurer's chivalrous but somewhat merciless soul, makes a better picture than does his more phlegmatic but brave and honourable antagonist, George Gering. Also in The Seats of the Mighty, Doltaire, the half-villain, overshadows the good English hero from first to last; and yet, despite the unconscious partiality for the individual in both books, English character and the English as a race, as a whole, are dominant in the narrative.

There is a long letter, as a dedication to this book, addressed to my father; there is a note also, which explains the spirit in which the book was written, and I have no desire to enlarge this introduction in the presence of these prefaces to the first edition. But I may say that this book was gravely important to me, because it was to test all my capacity for writing a novel with an historical background, and, as it were, in the custom of a bygone time. It was not really the first attempt at handling a theme belonging to past generations, because I had written for Good Words, about the year 1890, a short novel which I called The Chief Factor, a tale of the Hudson's Bay Company. It was the first novel or tale of mine which secured copyright under the new American copyright act of 1892.

There was a circumstance connected with this publication which is interesting. When I arrived in New York, I had only three days in which to have the book printed in order to secure the copyright before Good Words published the novel as its Christmas annual in its entirety. I tried Messrs. Harper & Brothers, and several other publishers by turn, but none of them could undertake to print the book in the time. At last some kind friend told me to go to the Trow Directory Binding Company, which I did. They said they could not print the story in the time. I begged them to reconsider. I told them how much was at stake for me. I said that I would stay in the office and read the proofs as they came from the press, and would not move until it was finished. Refusal had been written on the lips and the face of the manager at the beginning, but at last I prevailed. He brought the foreman down there and then. Each of us, elated by the conditions of the struggle, determined to pull the thing off. We printed that book of sixty-five thousand words or so, in forty-eight hours, and it arrived in Washington three hours before the time was up. I saved the copyright, and I need hardly say that my gratitude to the Trow Directory Binding Company was as great as their delight in having done a really brilliant piece of work.

The day after the copyright was completed, I happened to mention the incident to Mr. Archibald Clavering Gunter, author of Mr. Barnes of New York, who had a publishing house for his own books. He immediately made me an offer for The Chief Factor. I hesitated, because I had been dealing with great firms like Harpers, and, to my youthful mind, it seemed rather beneath my dignity to have the imprint of so new a firm as the Home

Publishing Company on the title-page of my book. I asked the advice of Mr. Walter H. Page, then editor of The Forum, now one of the proprietors of The World's Work and Country Life, and he instantly said: "What difference does it make who publishes your book? It is the public you want."

I did not hesitate any longer. The Chief Factor went to Mr. Archibald Clavering Gunter and the Home Publishing Company, and they made a very large sale of it. I never cared for the book however; it seemed stilted and amateurish, though some of its descriptions and some of its dialogues were, I think, as good as I can do; so, eventually, in the middle nineties, I asked Mr. Gunter to sell me back the rights in the book and give me control of it. This he did. I thereupon withdrew it from publication at once, and am not including it in this subscription edition. I think it better dead. But the writing of it taught me better how to write The Trail of the Sword; though, if I had to do this book again, I could construct it better.

I think it fresh and very vigorous, and I think it does not lack distinction, while a real air of romance--of refined romance--pervades it. But I know that Mr. W. E. Henley was right when, after most generously helping me to revise it, with a true literary touch wonderfully intimate and affectionate, he said to me: "It is just not quite big, but the next one will get home."

He was right. The Trail of the Sword is "just not quite," though I think it has charm; but it remained for The Seats of the Mighty to get home, as "W. E. H.", the most exacting, yet the most generous, of critics, said.

This book played a most important part in a development of my literary work, and the warm reception by the public--for in England it has been through its tenth edition, and in America through proportionate thousands-- was partly made possible by the very beautiful illustrations which accompanied its publication in The Illustrated London News. The artist was A. L. Forestier, and never before or since has my work received such distinguished pictorial exposition, save, perhaps, in The Weavers, when Andre Castaigne did such triumphant work. It is a joy still to look at the illustrations of The Trail of the Sword, for, absolutely faithful to the time, they add a note of verisimilitude to the tale.

A NOTE

THE actors in this little drama played their parts on the big stage of a new continent two hundred years ago. Despots sat upon the thrones of France and England, and their representatives on the Hudson and the St. Lawrence were despots too, with greater opportunity and to better ends. In Canada, Frontenac quarreled with his Intendant and his Council, set a stern hand upon the Church when she crossed with his purposes, cajoled, treated with, and fought the Indians by turn, and cherished a running quarrel with the English Governor of New York. They were striving for the friendship of the Iroquois on the one hand, and for the trade of the Great West on the other. The French, under such men as La Salle, had pushed their trading posts westward to the great lakes and beyond the Missouri, and north to the shores of Hudson's Bay. They traded and fought and revelled, hot with the spirit of adventure, the best of pioneers and the worst of colonists. Tardily, upon their trail, came the English and the Dutch, slow to acquire but strong to hold; not so rash in adventure, nor so adroit in intrigue, as fond of fighting, but with less of the gift of the woods, and much more the faculty for government. There was little interchange of friendliness and trade between the rival colonists; and Frenchmen were as rare on Manhattan Island as Englishmen on the heights of Quebec--except as prisoners.

G. P.

EPOCH THE FIRST

AN ENVOY EXTRAORDINARY

ONE summer afternoon a tall, good-looking stripling stopped in the midst of the town of New York, and asked his way to the governor's house. He attracted not a little attention, and he created as much astonishment when he came into the presence of the governor. He had been announced as an envoy from Quebec. "Some new insolence of the County Frontenac!" cried old Richard Nicholls, bringing his fist down on the table. For a few minutes he talked with his chamberfellow; then, "Show the gentleman in," he added. In the room without, the envoy from Quebec had stood flicking the dust from his leggings with a scarf. He was not more than eighteen, his face had scarcely an inkling of moustache, but he had an easy upright carriage, with an air of self-possession, the keenest of grey eyes, a strong pair of shoulders, a look of daring about his rather large mouth, which lent him a manliness well warranting his present service. He had been left alone, and the first thing he had done was to turn on his heel and examine the place swiftly. This he seemed to do mechanically, not as one forecasting danger, not as a spy. In the curve of his lips, in an occasional droop of his eyelids, there was a suggestion of humour: less often a quality of the young than of the old. For even in the late seven-teenth century, youth took itself seriously at times.

Presently, as he stood looking at the sunshine through the open door, a young girl came into the lane of light, waved her hand, with a little laugh, to some one in the distance, and stepped inside. At first she did not see him. Her glances were still cast back the way she had come. The young man could not follow her glance, nor was he anything curious. Young as he was, he could enjoy a fine picture. There was a pretty demureness in the girl's manner, a warm piquancy in the turn of the neck, and a delicacy in her gestures, which to him, fresh from hard hours in the woods, was part of some delightful Arcady--though Arcady was more in his veins than of his knowledge. For the young seigneur of New France spent far more hours with his gun than with his Latin, and knew his bush-ranging vassal better than his tutor; and this one was too complete a type of his order to reverse its record. He did not look to his scanty lace, or set himself seemingly; he did but stop flicking the scarf held loose in his fingers, his foot still on the bench. A smile played at his lips, and his eyes had a gleam of raillery. He heard the girl say in a soft, quaint voice, just as she turned towards him, "Foolish boy!" By this he knew that the pretty picture had for its inspiration one of his own sex.

She faced him, and gave a little cry of surprise. Then their eyes met. Immediately he made the most elaborate bow of all his life, and she swept a graceful courtesy. Her face was slightly flushed that this stranger should have seen, but he carried such an open, cordial look that she paused, instead of hurrying into the governor's room, as she had seemed inclined to do.

In the act the string of her hat, slung over her arm, came loose, and the hat fell to the floor. Instantly he picked it up and returned it. Neither had spoken a word. It seemed another act of the light pantomime at the door. As if they had both thought on the instant how droll it was, they laughed, and she said to him naively: "You have come to visit the governor? You are a Frenchman, are you not?"

To this in slow and careful English, "Yes," he replied; "I have come from Canada to see his excellency. Will you speak French?"

"If you please, no," she answered, smiling; "your English is better than my French. But I must go." And she turned towards the door of the governor's room.

"Do not go yet," he said. "Tell me, are you the governor's daughter?"

She paused, her hand at the door. "Oh no," she answered; then, in a sprightly way--"are you a governor's son?"

"I wish I were," he said, "for then there'd be a new intendant, and we'd put Nick Perrot in the council."

"What is an intendant?" she asked, "and who is Nick Perrot?"

"Bien! an intendant is a man whom King Louis appoints to worry the governor and the gentlemen of Canada, and to interrupt the trade. Nicolas Perrot is a fine fellow, and a great coureur du bois, and helps to get the governor out of troubles to-day, the intendant to-morrow. He is a splendid fighter. Perrot is my friend."

He said this, not with an air of boasting, but with a youthful and enthusiastic pride, which was relieved, by the twinkle in his eyes and his frank manner.

"Who brought you here?" she asked demurely. "Are they inside with the governor?"

He saw the raillery; though, indeed, it was natural to suppose that he had no business with the governor, but had merely come with some one. The question was not flattering. His hand went up to his chin a little awkwardly. She noted how large yet how well-shaped it was, or, rather, she remembered afterwards. Then it dropped upon the hilt of the rapier he wore, and he answered with good self-possession, though a little hot spot showed on his cheek: "The governor must have other guests who are no men of mine; for he keeps an envoy from Count Frontenac long in his anteroom."

The girl became very youthful indeed, and a merry light danced in her eyes and warmed her cheek. She came a step nearer. "It is not so? You do not come from Count Frontenac--all alone, do you?"

"I'll tell you after I have told the governor," he answered, pleased and amused.

"Oh, I shall hear when the governor hears," she answered, with a soft quaintness, and then vanished into the governor's chamber. She had scarce entered when the door opened again, and the servant, a Scotsman, came out to say that his excellency would receive him. He went briskly forward, but presently paused. A sudden sense of shyness possessed him. It was not the first time he had been ushered into vice-regal presence, but his was an odd position. He was in a strange land, charged with an embassy which accident had thrust upon him. Then, too, the presence of the girl had withdrawn him for an instant from the imminence of his duty. His youth came out of him, and in the pause one could fairly see him turn into man.

He had not the dark complexion of so many of his race, but was rather Saxon in face, with rich curling brown hair. Even in that brave time one might safely have bespoken for him a large career. And even while the Scotsman in the doorway eyed him with distant deprecation, as he eyed all

Frenchmen, good and bad, ugly or handsome, he put off his hesitation and entered the governor's chamber. Colonel Nicholls came forward to greet him, and then suddenly stopped, astonished. Then he wheeled upon the girl. "Jessica, you madcap!" he said in a low voice.

She was leaning against a tall chair, both hands grasping the back of it, her chin just level with the top. She had told the governor that Count Frontenac had sent him a lame old man, and that, enemy or none, he ought not to be kept waiting, with arm in sling and bandaged head. Seated at the table near her was a grave member of the governor's council, William Drayton by name. He lifted a reproving finger at her now, but with a smile on his kindly face, and "Fie, fie, young lady!" he said, in a whisper.

Presently the governor mastered his surprise, and seeing that the young man was of birth and quality, extended his hand cordially enough, and said: "I am glad to greet you, sir;" and motioned him to a seat. "But, pray, sit down," he added, "and let us hear the message Count Frontenac has sent. Meanwhile we would be favoured with your name and rank."

The young man thrust a hand into his doublet and drew forth a packet of papers. As he handed it over, he said in English--for till then the governor had spoken French, having once served with the army of France, and lived at the French Court: "Your excellency, my name is Pierre le Moyne of Iberville, son of Charles le Moyne, a seigneur of Canada, of whom you may have heard." (The governor nodded.) "I was not sent by Count Frontenac to you. My father was his envoy: to debate with you our trade in the far West and our dealings with the Iroquois."

"Exactly," said old William Drayton, tapping the table with his forefinger; "and a very sound move, upon my soul."

"Ay, ay," said the governor, "I know of your father well enough. A good fighter and an honest gentleman, as they say. But proceed, Monsieur le Moyne of Iberville."

"I am called Iberville," said the young man simply. Then: "My father and myself started from Quebec with good Nick Perrot, the coureur du bois--"

"I know him too," the governor interjected--"a scoundrel worth his weight in gold to your Count Frontenac."

"For whose head Count Frontenac has offered gold in his time," answered Iberville, with a smile.

"A very pretty wit," said old William Drayton, nodding softly towards the girl, who was casting bright, quizzical glances at the youth over the back of the chair.

Iberville went on: "Six days ago we were set upon by a score of your Indians, and might easily have left our scalps with them; but, as it chanced, my father was wounded, I came off scot-free, and we had the joy of ridding your excellency of half a dozen rogues."

The governor lifted his eyebrows and said nothing. The face of the girl over against the back of the chair had become grave.

"It was in question whether Perrot or I should bear Count Frontenac's message. Perrot knew the way, I did not; Perrot also knew the Indians."

"But Perrot," said the governor blufily, "would have been the letter- carrier; you are a kind of ambassador. Upon my soul, yes, a sort of ambassador!" he added, enjoying the idea; for, look at it how you would, Iberville was but a boy.

"That was my father's thought and my own," answered Iberville coolly. "There was my father to care for till his wound was healed and he could travel back to Quebec, so we thought it better Perrot should stay with him. A Le Moyne was to present himself, and a Le Moyne has done so."

The governor was impressed more deeply than he showed. It was a time of peace, but the young man's journey among Indian braves and English outlaws, to whom a French scalp was a thing of price, was hard and hazardous. His reply was cordial, then his fingers came to the seal of the packet; but the girl's hand touched his arm.

"I know his name," she said in the governor's ear, "but he does not know mine."

The governor patted her hand, and then rejoined: "Now, now, I forgot the lady; but I cannot always remember that you are full fifteen years old."

Standing up, with all due gravity and courtesy, "Monsieur Iberville," he said, "let me present you to Mistress Jessica Leveret, the daughter of my good and honoured and absent friend, the Honourable Hogarth Leveret."

So the governor and his councillor stood shoulder to shoulder at one window, debating Count Frontenac's message; and shoulder to shoulder at another stood Iberville and Jessica Leveret. And what was between these at that moment--though none could have guessed it--signified as much to the colonies of France and England, at strife in the New World, as the deliberations of their elders.

THE THREAT OF A RENEGADE

IBERVILLE was used to the society of women. Even as a young lad, his father's notable place in the colony, and the freedom and gaiety of life in Quebec and Montreal, had drawn upon him a notice which was as much a promise of the future as an accent of the present. And yet, through all of it, he was ever better inspired by the grasp of a common soldier, who had served with Carignan-Salieres, or by the greeting and gossip of such woodsmen as Du Lhut, Mantet, La Durantaye, and, most of all, his staunch friend Perrot, chief of the coureurs du bois. Truth is, in his veins was the strain of war and adventure first and before all. Under his tutor, the good Pere Dollier de Casson, he had never endured his classics, save for the sake of Hector and Achilles and their kind; and his knowledge of English, which his father had pressed him to learn,--for he himself had felt the lack of it in dealings with Dutch and English traders,--only grew in proportion as he was given Shakespeare and Raleigh to explore.

Soon the girl laughed up at him. "I have been a great traveller," she said, "and I have ears. I have been as far west as Albany and south to Virginia, with my father, who, perhaps you do not know, is in England now. And they told me everywhere that Frenchmen are bold, dark men, with great black eyes and very fine laces and wigs, and a trick of bowing and making foolish compliments; and they are not to be trusted, and they will not fight except in the woods, where there are trees to climb. But I see that it is not all true, for you are not dark, your eyes are not big or black, your laces are not much to see, you do not make compliments--"

"I shall begin now," he interrupted.

"--you must be trusted a little, or Count Frontenac would not send you, and--and--tell me, would you fight if you had a chance?"

No one of her sex had ever talked so to Iberville. Her demure raillery, her fresh, frank impertinence, through which there ran a pretty air of breeding, her innocent disregard of formality, all joined to impress him, to interest him. He was not so much surprised at the elegance and cleverness of her speech, for in Quebec girls of her age were skilled in languages and arts, thanks to the great bishop, Laval, and to Marie of the Incarnation. In response to her a smile flickered upon his lips. He had a quick fierce temper, but it had never been severely tried; and so well used was he to looking cheerfully upon things, so keen had been his zest in living, that, where himself was concerned, his vanity was not easily touched. So, looking with genial dryness, "You will hardly believe it, of course," he said, "but wings I have not yet grown, and the walking is bad 'twixt here and the Chateau St. Louis."

"Iroquois traps," she suggested, with a smile. "With a trick or two of English footpads," was his reply.

Meanwhile his eye had loitered between the two men in council at the farther window and the garden, into which he and the girl were looking. Presently he gave a little start and a low whistle, and his eyelids slightly drooped, giving him a handsome sulkiness. "Is it so?" he said between his teeth: "Radisson--Radisson, as I live!"

He had seen a man cross a corner of the yard. This man was short, dark-bearded, with black, lanky hair, brass earrings, and buckskin leggings, all the typical equipment of the French coureur du bois. Iberville had only got one glance at his face, but the sinister profile could never be forgotten. At once the man passed out of view. The girl had not seen him, she had been watching her companion. Presently she said, her fingers just brushing his sleeve, for he stood eyeing the point where the man had disappeared: "Wonderful! You look now as if you would fight. Oh, fierce, fierce as the governor when he catches a French spy!"

He turned to her and, with a touch of irony, "Pardon!" he retorted. "Now I shall look as blithe as the governor when a traitor deserts to him."

Of purpose he spoke loud enough to be heard by the governor and his friend. The governor turned sharply on him. He had caught the ring in the voice, that rash enthusiasm of eager youth, and, taking a step towards Iberville, Count Frontenac's letter still poised in his hand: "Were your words meant for my hearing, monsieur?" he said. "Were you speaking of me or of your governor?"

"I was thinking of one Radisson a traitor, and I was speaking of yourself, your excellency."

The governor had asked his question in French, in French the reply was given. Both the girl and Councillor Drayton followed with difficulty. Jessica looked a message to her comrade in ignorance. The old man touched the governor's arm. "Let it be in English if monsieur is willing. He speaks it well."

The governor was at work to hide his anger: he wished good greeting to Count Frontenac's envoy, and it seemed not fitting to be touched by the charges of a boy. "I must tell you frankly, Monsieur Iberville," he said, "that I do not choose to find a sort of challenge in your words; and I doubt that your father, had he been here, would have spoke quite so roundly. But I am for peace and happy temper when I can. I may not help it if your people, tired of the governance of Louis of France, come into the good ruling of King Charles. As for this man Radisson: what is it you would have?"

Iberville was now well settled back upon his native courage. He swallowed the rebuke with grace, and replied with frankness: "Radisson is an outlaw. Once he attempted Count Frontenac's life. He sold a band of our traders to the Iroquois. He led your Hollanders stealthily to cut off the Indians of the west, who were coming with their year's furs to our merchants. There is peace between your colony and ours--is it fair to harbour such a wretch in your court-yard? It was said up in Quebec, your excellency, that such men have eaten at your table."

During this speech the governor seemed choleric, but a change passed over him, and he fell to admiring the lad's boldness. "Upon my soul, monsieur," he said, "you are council, judge, and jury all in one; but I think I need not weigh the thing with you, for his excellency, from whom you come, has set forth this same charge,"--he tapped the paper,--"and we will not spoil good-fellowship by threshing it now." He laughed a little ironically. "And I promise you," he added, "that your Radisson shall neither drink wine nor eat bread with you at my table. And now, come, let us talk awhile together; for, lest any accident befall the packet you shall bear, I wish you to carry in your memory, with great distinctness, the terms of my writing to your governor. I would that it were not to be written, for I hate the quill, and I've seen the time I would rather point my sword red than my quill black."

By this the shadows were falling. In the west the sun was slipping down behind the hills, leaving the strong day with a rosy and radiant glamour, that faded away in eloquent tones to the grey, tinsel softness of the zenith. Out in the yard a sumach bush was aflame. Rich tiger-lilies thrust in at the sill, and lazy flies and king bees boomed in and out of the window. Something out of the sunset, out of the glorious freshness and primal majesty of the new land, diffused through the room where those four people stood, and made them silent. Presently the governor drew his chair to the table, and motioned Councillor Drayton and Iberville to be seated.

The girl touched his arm. "And where am I to sit?" she asked demurely. Colonel Nicholls pursed his lips and seemed to frown severely on her. "To sit? Why, in your room, mistress. Tut, tut, you are too bold. If I did not know your father was coming soon to bear you off, new orders should be issued. Yes, yes, e'en as I say," he added, as he saw the laughter in her eyes.

She knew that she could wind the big-mannered soldier about her finger. She had mastered his household; she was the idol of the settlement, her flexible intelligence, the flush of the first delicate bounty of womanhood had made him her slave. In a matter of vexing weight he would not have let her stay, but such deliberatings as he would have with Iberville could well bear her scrutiny. He reached out to pinch her cheek, but she deftly tipped her head and caught his outstretched fingers. "But where am I to sit?" she persisted. "Anywhere, then, but at the council-table," was his response, as he wagged a finger at her and sat down. Going over she perched herself on a high stool in the window behind Iberville. He could not see her, and, if he thought at all about it, he must have supposed that she could not see him. Yet she could; for against the window-frame was a mirror, and it reflected his face and the doings at the board. She did not listen to the rumble of voices. She fell to studying Iberville. Once or twice she laughed softly to herself.

As she turned to the window a man passed by and looked in at her. His look was singular, and she started. Something about his face was familiar. She found her mind feeling among far memories, for even the past of the young stretches out interminably. She shuddered, and a troubled look came into her eyes. Yet she could not remember. She leaned slightly forward, as if she were peering into that by-gone world which, maybe, is wider than the future for all of us--the past. Her eyes grew deep and melancholy. The sunset seemed to brighten around her all at once, and enmesh her in a golden web, burnishing her hair, and it fell across her brow with a peculiar radiance, leaving the temples in shadow, softening and yet lighting the carmine of her cheeks and lips, giving a feeling of life to her dress, which itself was like dusty gold. Her hands were caught and clasped at her knees. There was something spiritual and exalted in the picture. It had, too, a touch of tragedy, for something out of her nebulous past had been reflected in faint shadows in her eyes, and this again, by strange, delicate processes, was expressed in every line of her form, in all the aspect of her face. It was as if some knowledge were being filtered to her through myriad atmospheres of premonition; as though the gods in pity foreshadowed a great trouble, that the first rudeness of misery might be spared.

She did not note that Iberville had risen, and had come round the table to look over Councillor Drayton's shoulder at a map spread out. After standing a moment watching, the councillor's finger his pilot, he started back to his seat. As he did so he caught sight of her still in that poise of wonderment and sadness. He stopped short, then glanced at Colonel Nicholls and the councillor. Both were bent over the map, talking in eager tones. He came softly round the table, and was about to speak over her shoulder, when she drew herself up with a little shiver and seemed to come back from afar. Her hands went up to her eyes. Then she heard him. She turned quickly, with the pageant of her dreams still wavering in her face; smiled at him distantly, looked towards the window again in a troubled way, then stepped softly and swiftly to the door, and passed out. Iberville watched the door close and turned to the window. Again he saw, and this time nearer to the window, Radisson, and with him the man who had so suddenly mastered Jessica.

He turned to Colonel Nicholls. "Your excellency," he said, "will you not let me tell Count Frontenac that you forbid Radisson your purlieus? For, believe me, sir, there is no greater rogue unhanged, as you shall find some day to the hurt of your colony, if you shelter him."

The governor rose and paced the room thoughtfully. "He is proclaimed by Frontenac?" he asked.

"A price is on his head. As a Frenchman I should shoot him like a wolf where'er I saw him; and so I would now were I not Count Frontenac's ambassador and in your excellency's presence."

"You speak manfully, monsieur," said the governor, not ill-pleased; "but how might you shoot him now? Is he without there?" At this he came to where Iberville stood, and looked out. "Who is the fellow with him?" he asked.

"A cut-throat scoundrel, I'll swear, though his face is so smug," said Iberville. "What think you sir?" turning to the councillor, who was peering between their shoulders.

"As artless yet as strange a face as I have ever seen," answered the merchant. "What's his business here, and why comes he with the other rogue? He would speak with your excellency, I doubt not," he added.

Colonel Nicholls turned to Iberville. "You shall have your way," he said. "Yon renegade was useful when we did not know what sudden game was playing from Chateau St. Louis; for, as you can guess, he has friends as faithless as himself. But to please your governor, I will proclaim him."

He took his stick and tapped the floor. Waiting a moment, he tapped again. There was no sign. He opened the door; but his Scots body-guard was not in sight. "That's unusual," he said. Then, looking round: "Where is our other councillor? Gone?" he laughed. "Faith, I did not see her go. And now we can swear that where the dear witch is will Morris, my Scotsman, be found. Well, well! They have their way with us whether we will or no. But, here, I'll have your Radisson in at once."

He was in act to call when Morris entered. With a little hasty rebuke he gave his order to the man. "And look you, my good Morris," he added, "tell Sherlock and Weir to stand ready. I may need the show of firearms."

Turning to Iberville, he said: "I trust you will rest with us some days, monsieur. We shall have sports and junketings anon. We are not yet so grim as our friends in Massachusetts."

"I think I might venture two days with you, sir, if for nothing else, to see Radisson proclaimed. Count Frontenac would gladly cut months from his calendar to know you ceased to harbour one who can prove no friend," was the reply.

The governor smiled. "You have a rare taste for challenge, monsieur. To be frank, I will say your gift is more that of the soldier than the envoy. But upon my soul, if you will permit me, I think no less of you for that."

Then the door opened, and Morris brought in Radisson. The keen, sinister eyes of the woodsman travelled from face to face, and then rested savagely on Iberville. He scented trouble, and traced it to its source. Iberville drew back to the window and, resting his arm on the high stool where Jessica had sat, waited the event. Presently the governor came over to him.

"You can understand," he said quietly, "that this man has been used by my people, and that things may be said which--"

Iberville waved his hand respectfully. "I understand, your excellency," he said. "I will go." He went to the door.

The woodsman as he passed broke out: "There is the old saying of the woods, 'It is mad for the young wolf to trail the old bear.'"

"That is so," rejoined Iberville, with excellent coolness, "if the wolf holds not the spring of the trap."

In the outer room were two soldiers and the Scot. He nodded, passed into the yard, and there he paced up and down. Once he saw Jessica's face at a window, he was astonished to see how changed. It wore a grave, an apprehensive look. He fell to wondering, but, even as he wondered, his habit of observation made him take in every feature of the governor's house and garden, so that he could have reproduced all as it was mirrored in his eye. Presently he found himself again associating Radisson's comrade with the vague terror in Jessica's face. At last he saw the fellow come forth between two soldiers, and the woodsman turned his head from side to side, showing his teeth like a wild beast at sight of Iberville. His black brows twitched over his vicious eyes. "There are many ways to hell, Monsieur Iberville," he said. "I will show you one. Some day when you think you tread on a wisp of straw, it will be a snake with the deadly tooth. You have made an outlaw--take care! When the outlaw tires of the game, he winds it up quick. And some one pays for the candles and the cards."

Iberville walked up to him. "Radisson," he said in a voice well controlled, "you have always been an outlaw. In our native country you were a traitor; in this, you are the traitor still. I am not sorry for you, for you deserve not mercy. Prove me wrong. Go back to Quebec; offer to pay with your neck, then--"

"I will have my hour," said the woodsman, and started on.

"It's a pity," said Iberville to himself--"as fine a woodsman as Perrot, too!"

THE FACE AT THE WINDOW

AT the governor's table that night certain ladies and gentlemen assembled to do the envoy honour. There came, too, a young gentleman, son of a distinguished New Englander, his name George Gering, who was now in New York for the first time. The truth is, his visit was to Jessica, his old playmate, the mistress of his boyhood. Her father was in England, her mother had been dead many years, and Colonel Nicholls and his sister being kinsfolk, a whole twelvemonth ago she had been left with them. Her father had thought at first to house her with his old friend Edward Gering, but he loved the Cavalier-like tone of Colonel Nicholls's household better than the less inspiriting air which Madam Puritan Gering suffused about her home. Himself in early youth had felt the austerity of a Cavalier father turned a Puritan on a sudden, and he wished no such experience for his daughter. For all her abundancy of life and feeling, he knew how plastic and impressionable she was, and he dreaded to see that exaltation of her fresh spirit touched with gloom. She was his only child, she had been little out of his sight, her education had gone on under his own care, and, in so far as was possible in a new land, he had surrounded her with gracious influences. He looked forward to any definite separation (as marriage) with apprehension. Perhaps one of the reasons why he chose Colonel Nicholls's house for her home, was a fear lest George Gering should so impress her that she might somehow change ere his return. And in those times brides of sixteen were common as now they are rare.

She sat on the governor's left. All the brightness, the soft piquancy, which Iberville knew, had returned; and he wondered--fortunate to know that wonder so young--at her varying moods. She talked little, and most with the governor; but her presence seemed pervasive, the aura in her veins flowed from her eye and made an atmosphere that lighted even the scarred and rather sulky faces of two officers of His Majesty near. They had served with Nicholls in Spain, but not having eaten King Louis's bread, eyed all Frenchmen askance, and were not needlessly courteous to Iberville, whose achievements they could scarce appreciate, having done no Indian fighting.

Iberville sat at the governor's end, Gering at the other. It was noticed by Iberville that Gering's eyes were much on Jessica, and in the spirit of rivalry, the legitimate growth of race and habit, he began to speak to her with the air of easy but deliberate playfulness which marked their first meeting.

Presently she spoke across the table to him, after Colonel Nicholls had pledged him heartily over wine. The tone was a half whisper as of awe, in reality a pretty mockery. "Tell me," she said, "what is the bravest and greatest thing you ever did?"

"Jessica, Jessica!" said the governor in reproof. An old Dutch burgher laughed into his hand, and His Majesty's officers cocked their ears, for the whisper was more arresting than any loud talk. Iberville coloured, but the flush passed quickly and left him unembarrassed. He was not hurt, not even piqued, for he felt well used to her dainty raillery. But he saw that Gering's eyes were on him, and the lull that fell as by a common instinct-- for all could not have heard the question--gave him a thrill of timidity. But, smiling, he said drily across the table, his voice quiet and clear: "My bravest and greatest thing was to answer an English lady's wit in English."

A murmur of applause ran round, and Jessica laughed and clapped her hands. For the first time in his life Gering had a pang of jealousy and envy. Only that afternoon he had spent a happy hour with Jessica in the governor's garden, and he had then made an advance upon the simple relations of their life in Boston. She had met him without self-conscious- ness, persisting in her old ways, and showing only when she left him, and then for a breath, that she saw his new attitude. Now the eyes of the two men met, and Gering's dark face flushed and his brow lowered. Perhaps no one saw but Iberville, but he, seeing, felt a sudden desire to play upon the other's weakness. He was too good a sportsman to show temper in a game; he had suddenly come to the knowledge that love, too, is a game, and needs playing. By this time the dinner was drawing to its close and now a singular thing happened. As Jessica, with demure amusement, listened to the talk that followed Iberville's sally, she chanced to lift her eyes to a window. She started, changed colour, and gave a little cry. The governor's hand covered hers at once as he followed her look. It was a summer's night and the curtained windows were partly open. Iberville noted that Jessica's face wore the self-same shadow as in the afternoon when she had seen the stranger with Radisson.

"What was it, my dear?" said the governor.

She did not answer, but pressed his hand nervously. "A spy, I believe," said Iberville, in a low voice. "Yes, yes," said Jessica in a half whisper; "a man looked in at the window; a face that I have seen--but I can't remember when."

The governor went to the window and drew the curtains. There was nothing to see. He ordered Morris, who stood behind his chair, to have the ground searched and to bring in any straggler. Already both the officers were on their way to the door, and at this point it opened and let in a soldier. He said that as he and his comrade were returning from their duty with Radisson they saw a man lurking in the grounds and seized him. He had made no resistance, and was now under guard in the ante-room. The governor apologised to his guests, but the dinner could not be ended formally now, so the ladies rose and retired. Jessica, making a mighty effort to recover herself, succeeded so well that ere she went she was able to reproach herself for her alarm; the more so because the governor's sister showed her such consideration as would be given a frightened child-- and she had begun to feel something more.

The ladies gone, the governor drew his guests about him and ordered in the prisoner. Morris spoke up, saying that the man had begged an interview with the governor that afternoon, but, being told that his excellency was engaged, had said another hour would do. This man was the prisoner. He came in under guard, but he bore himself quietly enough and made a low bow to the governor. He was not an ill-favoured fellow. His eye was steely cold, but his face was hearty and round, and remarkably free from viciousness. He had a cheerful air and an alert freedom of manner, which suggested good-fellowship and honest enterprise.

Where his left hand had been was an iron hook, but not obtrusively in view, nor did it give any marked grimness to his appearance. Indeed, the effect was almost comical when he lifted it and scratched his head and then rubbed his chin with it; it made him look part bumpkin and part sailor. He bore the scrutiny of the company very well, and presently bowed again to the governor as one who waited the expression of that officer's goodwill and pleasure.

"Now, fellow," said the colonel, "think yourself lucky my soldiers here did not shoot you without shrift. You chance upon good-natured times. When a spying stranger comes dangling about these windows, my men are given to adorning the nearest tree with him. Out with the truth now. Who and what are you, and why are you here?"

The fellow bowed. "I am the captain of a little trading schooner, the Nell Gwynn, which anchors in the roadstead till I have laid some private business before your excellency and can get on to the Spanish Indies."

"Business--private business! Then what in the name of all that's infernal," quoth Nicholls, "brought your sneaking face to yon window to fright my lady-guests?" The memory of Jessica's alarm came hotly to his mind. "By Heaven," he said, "I have a will to see you lifted, for means to better manners."

The man stood very quiet, now and again, however, raising the hook to stroke his chin. He showed no fear, but Iberville, with his habit of observation, caught in his eyes, shining superficially with a sailor's open honesty, a strange ulterior look. "My business," so he answered Nicholls, "is for your excellency's ears." He bowed again.

"Have done with scraping. Now, I tell you what, my gentle spy, if your business hath not concern, I'll stretch you by your fingers there to our public gallows, and my fellows shall fill you with small shot as full as a pod of peas."

The governor rose and went into another room, followed by this strange visitor and the two soldiers. There he told the guard to wait at the door, which entered into the ante-room. Then he unlocked a drawer and took out of it a pair of pistols. These he laid on the table (for he knew the times), noting the while that the seaman watched him with a pensive, deprecating grin.

"Well, sir," he said sharply (for he was something nettled), "out with your business, and your name in preface."

"My name is Edward Bucklaw, and I have come to your excellency because I know there is no braver and more enterprising gentleman in the world." He paused. "So much for preamble; now for the discourse."

"By your excellency's leave. I am a poor man. I have only my little craft and a handful of seamen picked up at odd prices. But there's gold and silver enough I know of, owned by no man, to make cargo and ballast for the Nell Gwynn, or another twice her size."

"Gold and silver," said the governor, cocking his ear and eyeing his visitor up and down. Colonel Nicholls had an acquisitive instinct; he was interested. "Well, well, gold and silver," he continued, "to fill the Nell Gwynn and another! And what concern is that of mine? Let your words come plain off your tongue; I have no time for foolery."

"'Tis no foolery on my tongue, sir, as you may please to see."

He drew a paper from his pocket and shook it out as he came a little nearer, speaking all the while. His voice had gone low, running to a soft kind of chuckle, and his eyes were snapping with fire, which Iberville alone had seen was false. "I have come to make your excellency's fortune, if you will stand by with a good, stout ship and a handful of men to see me through."

The governor shrugged his shoulders. "Babble," he said, "all babble and bubble. But go on."

"Babble, your honour! Every word of it is worth a pint of guineas; and this is the pith of it. Far down West Indies way, some twenty-five, maybe, or thirty years ago, there was a plate ship wrecked upon a reef. I got it from a Spaniard, who had been sworn upon oath to keep it secret by priests who knew. The priests were killed and after a time the Spaniard died also, but not until he had given me the ways whereby I should get at what makes a man's heart rap in his weasand."

"Let me see your chart," said the governor.

A half-hour later he rose, went to the door, and sent a soldier for the two king's officers. As he did so, Bucklaw eyed the room doors, windows, fireplaces, with a grim, stealthy smile trailing across his face. Then suddenly the good creature was his old good self again--the comfortable shrewdness, the buoyant devil-may-care, the hook stroking the chin pensively. And the king's officers came in, and soon all four were busy with the map.

THE UPLIFTING OF THE SWORDS

IBERVILLE and Gering sat on with the tobacco and the wine. The older men had joined the ladies, the governor having politely asked them to do so when they chose. The other occupant of the room was Morris, who still stood stolidly behind his master's chair.

For a time he heard the talk of the two young men as in a kind of dream. Their words were not loud, their manner was amicable enough, if the sharing of a bottle were anything to the point. But they were sitting almost the full length of the table from him, and to quarrel courteously and with an air hath ever been a quality in men of gentle blood.

If Morris's eyesight had been better, he would have seen that Gering handled his wine nervously, and had put down his long Dutch pipe. He would also have seen that Iberville was smoking with deliberation, and drinking with a kind of mannered coolness. Gering's face was flushed, his fine nostrils were swelling viciously, his teeth showed white against his red lips, and his eyes glinted. There was a kind of devilry at Iberville's large and sensuous mouth, but his eyes were steady and provoking, and while Gering's words went forth pantingly, Iberville's were slow and concise, and chosen with the certainty of a lapidary.

It is hard to tell which had started the quarrel, but an edge was on their talk from the beginning. Gering had been moved by a boyish jealousy; Iberville, who saw the injustice of his foolish temper, had played his new-found enemy with a malicious adroitness. The aboriginal passions were strong in him. He had come of a people which had to do with essentials in the matter of emotions. To love, to hate, to fight, to explore, to hunt, to be loyal, to avenge, to bow to Mother Church, to honour the king, to beget children, to taste outlawry under a more refined name, and to die without whining: that was its range of duty, and a very sufficient range it was.

The talk had been running on Bucklaw. It had then shifted to Radisson. Gering had crowded home with flagrant emphasis the fact that, while Radisson was a traitor and a scoundrel,--which Iberville himself had admitted with an ironical frankness,--he was also a Frenchman. It was at this point that Iberville remembered, also with something of irony, the words that Jessica had used that afternoon when she came out of the sunshine into the ante-room of the governor's chamber. She had waved her hand into the distance and had said: "Foolish boy!" He knew very well that that part of the game was turned against him, but with a kind of cheerful recklessness, as was ever his way with odds against him, and he guessed that the odds were with Gering in the matter of Jessica,--he bent across the table and repeated them with an exasperating turn to his imperfect accent. "Foolish boy!" he said, and awaited, not for long, the event.

"A fool's lie," retorted Gering, in a low, angry voice, and spilled his wine.

At that Iberville's heart thumped in his throat with anger, and the roof of his mouth became dry; never in his life had he been called a liar. The first time that insult strikes a youth of spirit he goes a little mad.

But he was very quiet--an ominous sort of quietness, even in a boy. He got to his feet and leaned over the table, speaking in words that dropped on the silence like metal: "Monsieur, there is but one answer."

At this point Morris, roused from his elaborate musings, caught, not very clearly, at the meaning of it all. But he had not time to see more, for just then he was called by the governor, and passed into the room where Mammon, for the moment, perched like a leering, little dwarf upon the shoulders of adventurous gentlemen grown avaricious on a sudden.

"Monsieur, there is but one way. Well?" repeated Iberville.

"I am ready," replied Gering, also getting to his feet. The Frenchman was at once alive to certain difficulties. He knew that an envoy should not fight, and that he could ask no one to stand his second; also that it would not be possible to arrange a formal duel between opposites so young as Gering and himself. He sketched this briefly, and the Bostonian nodded moody assent. "Come, then," said Iberville, "let us find a place. My sword is at my hand. Yours?"

"Mine is not far off," answered Gering sullenly. Iberville forbore to point a moral, but walked to the mantel, above which hung two swords of finest steel, with richly-chased handles. He had noted them as soon as he had entered the room. "By the governor's leave," he said, and took them down. "Since we are to ruffle him let him furnish the spurs--eh? Shall we use these, and so be even as to weapons? But see," he added, with a burst of frankness, "I am in a--a trouble." It was not easy on the instant to find the English word. He explained the duties of his mission. It was singular to ask his enemy that he should see his papers handed to Count Frontenac if he were killed, but it was characteristic of him.

"I will see the papers delivered," said Gering, with equal frankness.

"That is, if by some miraculous chance I should be killed," added Iberville. "But I have other ends in view."

"I have only one end in view," retorted Gering. "But wait," he said, as they neared the door leading into the main hall; "we may be seen. There is another way into the grounds through a little hall here." He turned and opened a door almost as small as a panel. "I was shown this secret door the other day, and since ours is a secret mission let us use it."

"Very well. But a minute more," said Iberville. He went and unhooked a fine brass lantern, of old Dutch workmanship, swung from the ceiling by a chain. "We shall need a light," he remarked.

They passed into the musty little hallway, and Gering with some difficulty drew back the bolts. The door creaked open and they stepped out into the garden,

Iberville leading the way. He had not conned his surroundings that afternoon for nothing, and when they had reached a quiet place among some firs he hung the lantern to the branch of a tree, opening the little ornamental door so that the light streamed out. There was not much of it, but it would serve, and without a word, like two old warriors, they took off their coats.

Meanwhile Morris had returned to the dining-room to find Jessica standing agaze there. She had just come in; for, chancing to be in her bed-chamber, which was just over the secret hallway, she had heard Gering shoot the bolts. Now, the chamber was in a corner, so that the window faced another way, but the incident seemed strange to her, and she stood for a moment listening. Then hearing the door shut, she ran down the stairs, knocked at the dining-room door and, getting no answer, entered, meeting Morris as he came from the governor's room.

"Morris, Morris," she said, "where are they all?"

"The governor is in his room, mistress."

"Who are with him?" He told her.

"Where are the others?" she urged. "Mr. Gering and Monsieur Iberville -- where are they?"

The man's eyes had flashed to the place where the swords were used to hang. "Lord God!" he said under his breath.

Her eyes had followed his. She ran forward to the wall and threw up her hands against it. "Oh Morris," she said distractedly, "they have taken the swords!" Then she went past him swiftly through the panel and the outer door. She glanced around quickly, running, as she did so, with a kind of blind instinct towards the clump of firs. Presently she saw a little stream of light in the trees. Always a creature of abundant energy and sprightliness, she swept through the night, from the comedy behind to the tragedy in front; the grey starlight falling about her white dress and making her hair seem like a cloud behind her as she ran. Suddenly she came in on the two sworders with a scared, transfigured face.

Iberville had his man at an advantage, and was making the most of it when she came in at an angle behind the other, and the sight of her stayed his arm. It was but for a breath, but it served. Gering had not seen, and his sword ran up Iberville's arm, making a little trench in the flesh.

She ran in on them from the gloom, saying in a sharp, aching voice: "Stop, stop! Oh, what madness!" The points dropped and they stepped back. She stood between them, looking from one to the other. At that moment Morris burst in also. "In God's name," he said, "is this your honouring of the king's governor! Ye that have eat and drunk at his table the night! Have ye nae sense o' your manhood, young gentlemen, that for a mad gossip ower the wine ye wend into the dark to cut each other's throats?

Think--think shame, baith o' ye, being as ye are of them that should know better."

Gering moodily put on his coat and held his peace. Iberville tossed his sword aside, and presently wrung the blood from his white sleeve. The girl saw him, and knew that he was wounded. She snatched a scarf from her waist and ran towards him. "You are wounded," she said. "Oh, take this!"

"I am so much sorry, indeed," he answered coolly, winding the scarf about his arm. "Mistress Leveret came too soon."

His face wore a peculiar smile, but his eyes burned with anger; his voice was not excited. Immediately, however, as he looked at Jessica, his mood seemed to change.

"Morris," he said, "I am sorry. Mademoiselle," he added, "pardon! I regret whatever gives you pain." Gering came near to her, and Iberville could see that a flush stole over Jessica's face as he took her hand and said: "I am sorry--that you should have known."

"Good!" said Iberville, under his breath. "Good! he is worth fighting again."

A moment afterwards Morris explained to them that if the matter could be hushed he would not impart it to the governor--at least, not until Iberville had gone. Then they all started back towards the house. It did not seem incongruous to Iberville and Gering to walk side by side; theirs was a superior kind of hate. They paused outside the door, on Morris's hint, that he might see if the coast was clear, and return the swords to their place on the wall.

Jessica turned in the doorway. "I shall never forgive you," she said, and was swallowed by the darkness. "Which does she mean?" asked Iberville, with a touch of irony. The other was silent.

In a moment Morris came back to tell them that they might come, for the dining-room was empty still.

THE FRUITS OF THE LAW

BUCKLAW having convinced the governor and his friends that down in the Spaniards' country there was treasure for the finding, was told that he might come again next morning. He asked if it might not be late afternoon instead, because he had cargo from the Indies for sale, and in the morning certain merchants were to visit his vessel. Truth to tell he was playing a deep game. He wanted to learn the governor's plans for the next afternoon and evening, and thought to do so by proposing this same change. He did not reckon foolishly. The governor gave him to understand that there would be feasting next day: first, because it was the birthday of the Duke of York; secondly, because it was the anniversary of the capture from the Dutch; and, last of all, because there were Indian chiefs to come from Albany to see New York and himself for the first time. The official celebration would begin in the afternoon and last till sundown, so that all the governor's time must be fully occupied. But Bucklaw said, with great candour, that unfortunately he had to sail for Boston within thirty-six hours, to keep engagements with divers assignees for whom he had special cargo. If his excellency, he said, would come out to his ship the next evening when the shows were done, he would be proud to have him see his racketing little craft; and it could then be judged if, with furbishing and armaments, she could by any means be used for the expedition. Nicholls consented, and asked the king's officers if they would accompany him. This they were exceedingly glad to do: so that the honest shipman's good nature and politeness were vastly increased, and he waved his hook in so funny and so boyish a way it set them all a-laughing.

So it was arranged forthwith that he should be at a quiet point on the shore at a certain hour to row the governor and his friends to the Nell Gwynn. And, this done, he was bade to go to the dining-room and refresh himself.

He obeyed with cheerfulness, and was taken in charge by Morris, who, having passed on Iberville and Gering to the drawing-room, was once more at his post, taciturn as ever. The governor and his friends had gone straight to the drawing-room, so that Morris and he were alone. Wine was set before the sailor and he took off a glass with gusto, his eye cocked humorously towards his host. "No worse fate for a sinner," quoth he; "none better for a saint."

Morris's temper was not amiable. He did not like the rascal. "Ay," said he, "but many's the sinner has wished yon wish, and footed it from the stocks to the gallows."

Bucklaw laughed up at him. It was not a pretty laugh, and his eyes were insolent and hard. But that, changed almost on the instant. "A good thrust, mighty Scot," he said. "Now what say you to a pasty, or a strip of beef cut where the juice runs, and maybe the half of a broiled fowl?"

Morris, imperturbably deliberate, left the room to seek the kitchen. Bucklaw got instantly to his feet. His eye took in every window and door, and ran along the ceiling and the wall. There was a sudden click in the wall before him. It was the door leading to the unused hallway, which had not been properly closed and had sprung open. He caught up a candle, ran over, entered the hallway, and gave a grunt of satisfaction. He hastily and softly drew the bolts of the outer door, so that any one might come in from the garden, then stepped back into the dining-room and closed the panel tight behind him, remarking with delight that it had no spring-lock, and could be opened from the hallway. He came back quickly to the table, put down the candle, took his seat, stroked his chin with his hook, and chuckled. When Morris came back, he was holding his wine with one hand while he hummed a snatch of song and drummed lightly on the table with the hook. Immediately after came a servant with a tray, and the Scotsman was soon astonished, not only at the buxomness of his appetite, but at the deftness with which he carved and handled things with what he called his "tiger." And so he went on talking and eating, and he sat so long that Jessica, as she passed into the corridor and up the stairs, wearied by the day, heard his voice uplifted in song. It so worked upon her that she put her hands to her ears, hurried to her room, and threw herself upon the bed in a distress she could set down to no real cause.

Before the governor and his guests parted for the night, Iberville, as he made his adieus to Gering, said in a low voice: "The same place and time to-morrow night, and on the same conditions?"

"I shall be happy," said Gering, and they bowed with great formality.

The governor had chanced to hear a word or two and, thinking it was some game of which they spoke, said: "Piquet or a game of wits, gentlemen?"

"Neither, your excellency," quoth Gering--"a game called fox and goose."

"Good," said Iberville, under his breath; "my Puritan is waking."

The governor was in ripe humour. "But it is a game of wits, then, after all. Upon my soul, you two should fence like a pair of veterans."

"Only for a pass or two," said Iberville dryly. "We cannot keep it up."

All this while a boat was rowing swiftly from the shore of the island towards a craft carrying Nell Gwynn beneath the curious, antique figure-head. There were two men in her, and they were talking gloatingly and low.

"See, bully, how I have the whole thing in my hands. Ha! Received by the governor and his friends! They are all mad for the doubloons, which are not for them, my Radisson, but for you and me, and for a greater than Colonel Richard Nicholls. Ho, ho! I know him--the man who shall lead the hunt and find the gold--the only man in all that cursed Boston whose heart I would not eat raw, so help me Judas! And his name--no. That is to come. I will make him great."

Again he chuckled. "Over in London they shall take him to their bosoms. Over in London his blessed majesty shall dub him knight--treasure-trove is a fine reason for the touch of a royal sword--and the king shall say: 'Rise, Sir William'--No, it is not time for the name; but it is not Richard Nicholls, it is not Hogarth Leveret." He laughed like a boy. "I have you, Hogarth Leveret, in my hand, and by God I will squeeze you until there is a drop of heart's blood at every pore of your skin!"

Now and again Radisson looked sideways at him, a sardonic smile at his lip. At last: "Bien," he said, "you are merry. So--I shall be merry too, for I have scores to wipe away, and they shall be wiped clean-- clean."

"You are with me, then," the pirate asked; "even as to the girl?"

"Even as to the girl," was the reply, with a brutal oath.

"That is good, dear lad. Blood of my soul, I have waited twelve years-- twelve years."

"You have not told me," rejoined the Frenchman; "speak now."

"There is not much to tell, but we are to be partners once and for all. See, my beauty. He was a kite-livered captain. There was gold on board. We mutinied and put him and four others--their livers were like his own-- in a boat with provisions plenty. Then we sailed for Boston. We never thought the crew of skulkers would reach land, but by God they drifted in again the very hour we found port. We were taken and condemned. First, I was put into the stocks, hands and feet, till I was fit for the pillory; from the pillory to the wooden horse." Here he laughed, and the laugh was soft and womanlike. "Then the whipping-post, when I was made pulp from my neck to my loins. After that I was to hang. I was the only one they cooked so; the rest were to hang raw. I did not hang; I broke prison and ran. For years I was a slave among the Spaniards. Years more--in all, twelve--and then I came back with the little chart for one thing, this to do for another. Who was it gave me that rogues' march from the stocks to the gallows's foot? It was Hogarth Leveret, who deals out law in Massachusetts in the king's name, by the grace of God. It was my whim to capture him and take him on a journey--such a journey as he would go but once. Blood of my soul, the dear lad was gone. But there was his child. See this: when I stood in the pillory a maid one day brought the child to the foot of the platform, lifted it up in her arms and said: 'Your father put that villain there.' That woman was sister to one of the dogs we'd set adrift. The child stared at me hard, and I looked at her, though my eyes were a little the worse for wear, so that she cried out in great fright--the sweet innocent! and then the wench took her away. When she saw my face to-night--to-day--it sent her wild, but she did not remember." He rubbed his chin in ecstasy and drummed his knee. "Ha! I cannot have the father--so I'll have the goodly child, and great will be the ransom. Great will be the ransom, my Fren- chman!" And once more he tapped Radisson with the tiger.

THE KIDNAPPING

THE rejoicing had reached its apogee, and was on the wane. The Puritan had stretched his austereness to the point of levity; the Dutchman had comfortably sweated his obedience and content; the Cavalier had paced it with a pretty air of patronage and an eye for matron and maid; the Indian, come from his far hunting-grounds, bivouacked in the governor's presence as the pipe of peace went round.

About twilight the governor and his party had gone home. Deep in ceremonial as he had been, his mind had run upon Bucklaw and the Spaniards' country. So, when the dusk was growing into night, the hour came for his visit to the Nell Gwynn. With his two soldier friends and Councillor Drayton, he started by a roundabout for the point where he looked to find Bucklaw. Bucklaw was not there: he had other fish to fry, and the ship's lights were gone. She had changed her anchorage since afternoon.

"It's a bold scheme," Bucklaw was saying to his fellow-ruffian in the governor's garden, "and it may fail, yet 'twill go hard, but we'll save our skins. No pluck, no pence. Once again, here's the trick of it. I'll go in by the side door I unlocked last night, hide in the hallway, then enter the house quietly or boldly, as the case may be. Plan one: a message from his excellency to Miss Leveret, that he wishes her to join him on the Nell Gwynn. Once outside it's all right. She cannot escape us. We have our cloaks and we have the Spanish drug. Plan two: make her ours in the house. Out by this hall door--through the grounds--to the beach--the boat in waiting--and so, up anchor and away! Both risky, as you see, but the bolder the game the sweeter the spoil. You're sure her chamber is above the hallway, and that there's a staircase to it from the main hall?"

"I am very well sure. I know the house up-stairs and down."

Bucklaw looked to his arms. He was about starting on his quest when they heard footsteps, and two figures appeared. It was Iberville and Gering. They paused a moment not far from where the rogues were hid.

"I think you will agree," said Iberville, "that we must fight."

"I have no other mind."

"You will also be glad if we are not come upon, as last night; though, confess, the lady gave you a lease of life?"

"If she comes to-night, I hope it will be when I have done with you," answered Gering.

Iberville laughed a little, and the laugh had fire in it--hatred, and the joy of battle. "Shall it be here or yonder in the pines, where we were in train last night?"

"Yonder."

"So." Then Iberville hummed ironically a song:

> "Oh, bury me where I have fought and fallen,
> Your scarf across my shoulder, lady mine."

They passed on. "The game is in our hands," said Bucklaw. "I understand this thing. That's a pair of gallant young sprigs, but the choice is your Frenchman, Radisson."

"I'll pink his breast-bone full of holes if the other doesn't-- curse him."

A sweet laugh trickled from Bucklaw's lips like oil. "That's neither here nor there. I'd like to have him down Acapulco way, dear lad. . . And now, here's my plan all changed. I'll have my young lady out to stop the duel, and, God's love, she'll come alone. Once here she's ours, and they may cut each other's throats as they will, sweetheart."

He crossed the yard, tried the door,--unlocked, as he had left it,-- pushed it open, and went in, groping his way to the door of the dining-room. He listened, and there was no sound. Then he heard some one go in. He listened again. Whoever it was had sat down. Very carefully he felt for the spring and opened the door. Jessica was seated at the table with paper and an ink-horn before her. She was writing. Presently she stopped--the pen was bad. She got up and went away to her room. Instantly Bucklaw laid his plan. He entered as she disappeared, went to the table and looked at the paper on which she had been writing. It bore but the words, "Dear Friend." He caught up the quill and wrote hurriedly beneath them, this:

"If you'd see two gentlemen fighting, go now where you stopped them last night. The wrong one may be killed unless."

With a quick flash of malice he signed, in half a dozen lightning-like strokes, with a sketch of his hook. Then he turned, hurried into the little hall, and so outside, and posted himself beside a lilac bush, drawing down a bunch of the flowers to drink in their perfume. Jessica, returning, went straight to the table. Before she sat down she looked up to the mantel, but the swords were there. She sighed, and a tear glistened on her eyelashes. She brushed it away with her dainty fingertips and, as she sat down, saw the paper. She turned pale, caught it up, read it with a little cry, and let it drop with a shudder of fear and dismay. She looked round the room. Everything was as she had left it. She was dazed. She stared at the paper again, then ran and opened the panel through which Bucklaw had passed, and found the outer door ajar. With a soft, gasping moan she passed into the garden, went swiftly by the lilac bush and on towards the trees. Bucklaw let her do so; it was his design that she should be some way from the house. But, hidden by the bushes, he was running almost parallel with her. On the other side of her was Radisson, also running. She presently heard them and swerved, poor child, into the gin of the fowler! But as the cloak was thrown over her head she gave a cry.

The firs, where Iberville and Gering had just plucked out their swords, were not far, and both men heard. Gering, who best knew the voice, said hurriedly: "It is Jessica!"

Without a word Iberville leaped to the open, and came into it ahead of Gering. They saw the kidnappers and ran. Iberville was the first to find what Bucklaw was carrying. "Mother of God," he called, "they're taking her off!"

"Help! help!" cried Gering, and they pushed on. The two ruffians were running hard, but it had been an unequal race at the best, and Jessica lay unconscious in Bucklaw's arms, a dead weight. Presently they plunged into the bushes and disappeared. Iberville and Gering passed through the bushes also, but could neither see nor hear the quarry. Gering was wild with excitement and lost his presence of mind. Meanwhile Iberville went beating for a clue. He guessed that he was dealing with good woodsmen, and that the kidnappers knew some secret way out of the garden. It was so. The Dutch governor had begun to build an old-fashioned wall with a narrow gateway, so fitted as to seem part of it. Through this the two had vanished.

Iberville was almost in despair. "Go back," he suddenly said to Gering, "and rouse the house and the town. I will get on the trail again if I can."

Gering started away. In this strange excitement their own foolish quarrel was forgotten, and the stranger took on himself to command; he was, at least, not inexperienced in adventure and the wiles of desperate men. All at once he came upon the wall. He ran along it, and presently his fingers felt the passage. An instant and he was outside and making for the shore, in the sure knowledge that the ruffians would take to the water. He thought of Bucklaw, and by some impossible instinct divined the presence of his hand. Suddenly he saw something flash on the ground. He stooped and picked it up. It was a shoe with a silver buckle. He thrilled to the finger-tips as he thrust it in his bosom and pushed on. He was on the trail now. In a few moments he came to the waterside. He looked to where he had seen the Nell Gwynn in the morning, and there was never a light in view. Then a twig snapped, and Bucklaw, the girl in his arms, came bundling out of the trees upon the bank. He had sent Radisson on ahead to warn his boat's crew.

He saw Iberville as soon as Iberville saw him. He knew that the town would be roused by this time and the governor on fire for revenge. But there was nothing for it but fight. He did not fear the result. Time was life to him, and he swung the girl half behind him with his hook-hand as Iberville came on, and, whipping out his hanger, caught the Frenchman's thrust. Instantly he saw that his opposite was a swordsman, so he let the girl slip to the ground, and suddenly closing with Iberville, lunged desperately and expertly at him, straight for a mortal part. But the Frenchman was too agile and adroit for him: he took the thrust in the flesh of his ribs and riposted like lightning. The pirate staggered back, but pulled himself together instantly, lunged, and took his man in the flesh of his upper sword arm. Iberville was bleeding from the wound in his side and slightly stiff from the slash of the night before, but every fibre of his hurt body was on the defensive. Bucklaw knew it, and seemed to debate if the game were worth the candle. The town was afoot, and he had earned a halter for his pains. He was by no means certain that he could kill this champion and carry off the girl. Moreover, he did not want Iberville's life, for such devils have their likes and dislikes, and he had fancied the chivalrous youngster from the first. But he doubted only for an instant. What was such a lad's life compared with his revenge? It was madness, as he knew, for a shot would guide the pursuit: none the less, did he draw a pistol from his belt and fire. The bullet grazed the lad's temple, carrying away a bit of his hair. Iberville staggered forwards, so weak was he from loss of blood, and, with a deep instinct of protection and preservation, fell at Jessica's feet. There was a sound of footsteps and crackling of brush. Bucklaw stooped to pick up his prey, but a man burst on him from the trees. He saw that the game was up and he half raised his knife, but that was only the mad rage of the instant. His revenge did not comprise so unheard-of a crime. He thought he had killed Iberville: that was enough. He sprang away towards the spot where his comrades awaited him. Escape was his sole ambition now. The new-comer ran forwards, and saw the boy and girl lying as they were dead. A swift glance at Iberville, and he slung his musket shoulderwards and fired at the retreating figure. It was a chance shot, for the light was bad and Bucklaw was already indistinct.

Now the man dropped on his knee and felt Iberville's heart. "Alive!" he said. "Alive, thank the mother of God! Mon brave! It is ever the same -- the great father, the great son."

As he withdrew his hand it brushed against the slipper. He took it out, glanced at it, and turned to the cloaked figure. He undid the cloak and saw Jessica's pale face. He shook his head. "Always the same," he said, "always the same: for a king, for a friend, for a woman! That is the Le Moyne."

But he was busy as he spoke. With the native chivalry of the woodsman, he cared first for the girl. Between her lips he thrust his drinking- horn and held her head against his shoulder.

"My little ma'm'selle-ma'm'selle!" he said. "Wake up. It is nothing-- you are safe. Ah, the sweet lady! Come, let me see the colour of your eyes. Wake up--it is nothing."

Presently the girl did open her eyes. He put the drinking-horn again to her lips. She shuddered and took a sip, and then, invigorated, suddenly drew away from him. "There, there," he said; "it is all right. Now for my poor Iberville." He took Iberville's head to his knee and thrust the drinking-horn between his teeth, as he had done with Jessica, calling him in much the same fashion. Iberville came to with a start. For a moment he stared blindly at his rescuer, then a glad intelligence flashed into his eyes.

"Perrot! dear Nick Perrot!" he cried. "Oh, good--good," he added softly. Then with sudden anxiety:

"Where is she? Where is she?"

"I am safe, monsieur," Jessica said gently; "but you--you are wounded." She came over and dropped on her knees beside him.

"A little," he said; "only a little. You cared for her first?" he asked of Perrot.

Perrot chuckled. "These Le Moynes!" he said: under his breath. Then aloud: "The lady first, monsieur."

"So," answered Iberville. "And Bucklaw--the devil, Bucklaw?"

"If you mean the rogue who gave you these," said Perrot, touching the wounds, which he had already begun to bind, "I think he got away--the light was bad."

Jessica would have torn her frock for a bandage, but Perrot said in his broken English: "No, pardon. Not so. The cloak la-bas."

She ran and brought it to him. As she did so Perrot glanced down at her feet, and then, with a touch of humour, said: "Pardon, but you have lost your slipper, ma'm'selle?"

He foresaw the little comedy, which he could enjoy even in such painful circumstances.

"It must have dropped off," said Jessica, blushing. "But it does not matter."

Iberville blushed too, but a smile also flitted across his lips. "If you will but put your hand into my waistcoat here," he said to her, "you will find it." Timidly she did as she was bid, drew forth the slipper, and put it on.

"You see," said Iberville, still faint from loss of blood, "a Frenchman can fight and hunt too--hunt the slipper."

Suddenly a look of pain crossed her face.

"Mr. Gering, you--you did not kill him?" she asked. "Oh no, mademoiselle," said Iberville; "you stopped the game again."

Presently he told her what had happened, and how Gering was rousing the town. Then he insisted upon getting on his feet, that they might make their way to the governor's house. Stanchly he struggled on, his weight upon Perrot, till presently he leaned a hand also on Jessica's shoulder-she had insisted. On the way, Perrot told how it was he chanced to be there. A band of coureurs du bois, bound for Quebec, had come upon old Le Moyne and himself in the woods. Le Moyne had gone on with these men, while Perrot pushed on to New York, arriving at the very moment of the kidnapping. He heard the cry and made towards it. He had met Gering, and the rest they knew.

Certain things did not happen. The governor of New York did not at once engage in an expedition to the Spaniards' country. A brave pursuit was made, but Bucklaw went uncaptured. Iberville and Gering did not make a third attempt to fight; Perrot prevented that. Iberville left, however, with a knowledge of three things: that he was the first Frenchman from Quebec who had been, or was likely to be, popular in New York; that Jessica Leveret had shown a tender gratitude towards him--naive, candid-- which set him dreaming gaily of the future; that Gering and he, in spite of outward courtesy, were still enemies; for Gering could not forget that, in the rescue of Jessica, Iberville had done the work while he merely played the crier.

"We shall meet again, monsieur," said Iberville at last; "at least, I hope so."

"I shall be glad," answered Gering mechanically. "But 'tis like I shall come to you before you come to me," added Iberville, with meaning. Jessica was standing not far away, and Gering did not instantly reply. In the pause, Iberville said: "Au revoir! A la bonne heure!" and walked away. Presently he turned with a little ironical laugh and waved his hand at Gering; and laugh and gesture rankled in Gering for many a day.

EPOCH THE SECOND

FRIENDS IN COUNCIL

MONTREAL and Quebec, dear to the fortunes of such men as Iberville, were as cheerful in the still iron winter as any city under any more cordial sky then or now: men loved, hated, made and broke bargains, lied to women, kept a foolish honour with each other, and did deeds of valour for a song, as ever they did from the beginning of the world. Through the stern soul of Nature ran the temperament of men who had hearts of summer; and if, on a certain notable day in Iberville's life, one could have looked through the window of a low stone house in Notre Dame Street, Montreal, one could have seen a priest joyously playing a violin; though even in Europe, Maggini and Stradivarius were but little known, and the instrument itself was often called an invention of the devil.

The room was not ornamented, save by a crucifix, a pleasant pencil-drawing of Bishop Laval, a gun, a pair of snow-shoes, a sword, and a little shrine in one corner, wherein were relics of a saint. Of necessaries even there were few. They were unremarkable, save in the case of two tall silver candlesticks, which, with their candles at an angle from the musician, gave his face strange lights and shadows.

The priest was powerfully made; so powerful indeed, so tall was he, that when, in one of the changes of the music, a kind of exaltation filled him, and he came to his feet, his head almost touched the ceiling. His shoulders were broad and strong, and though his limbs were hid by his cassock, his arms showed almost huge, and the violin lay tucked under his chin like a mere toy. In the eye was a penetrating but abstracted look, and the countenance had the gravity of a priest lighted by a cheerful soul within. It had been said of Dollier de Casson that once, attacked by two renegade Frenchmen, he had broken the leg of one and the back of the other, and had then picked them up and carried them for miles to shelter and nursing. And it was also declared by the romantic that the man with the broken back recovered, while he with the shattered leg, recovering also, found that his foot, pointing backwards, "made a fool of his nose."

The Abbe de Casson's life had one affection, which had taken the place of others, now almost lost in the distance of youth, absence, and indifference.

For France lay far from Montreal, and the priest-musician was infinitely farther off: the miles which the Church measures between the priest and his lay boyhood are not easily reckoned. But such as Dollier de Casson must have a field for affection to enrich. You cannot drive the sap of the tree in upon itself. It must come out or the tree must die-burst with the very misery of its richness.

This night he was crowding into the music four years of events: of memory, hope, pride, patience, and affection. He was waiting for some one whom he had not seen for these four years. Time passed. More and more did the broad sonorous notes fill the room. At length they ceased, and with a sigh he pressed the violin once, twice, thrice to his lips.

"My good Stradivarius," he said, "my pearless one!" Once again he kissed it, and then, drawing his hand across his eyes, he slowly wrapped the violin in a velvet cloth, put it away in an iron box, and locked it up. But presently he changed his mind, took it out again, and put it on the table, shaking his head musingly.

"He will wish to see it, maybe to hear it," he said half aloud.

Then he turned and went into another room. Here there was a prie-dieu in a corner, and above it a crucifix. He knelt and was soon absorbed.

For a time there was silence. At last there was a crunching of moccasined feet upon the crisp snow, then a slight tap at the outer door, and immediately it was opened. A stalwart young man stepped inside. He looked round, pleased, astonished, and glanced at the violin, then meaningly towards the nearly closed door of the other room. After which he pulled off his gloves, threw his cap down, and with a significant toss of the head, picked up the violin.

He was a strong, handsome man of about twenty-two, with a face at once open and inscrutable: the mouth with a trick of smiling, the eyes fearless, convincing, but having at the same time a look behind this--an alert, profound speculation, which gave his face singular force. He was not so tall as the priest in the next room, but still he was very tall, and every movement had a lithe, supple strength. His body was so firm that, as he bent or turned, it seemed as of soft flexible metal.

Despite his fine manliness, he looked very boylike as he picked up the violin, and with a silent eager laugh put it under his chin, nodding gaily, as he did so, towards the other room. He bent his cheek to the instrument--almost as brown as the wood itself--and made a pass or two in the air with the bow, as if to recall a former touch and tune. A satisfied look shot up in his face, and then with an almost impossible softness he drew the bow across the strings, getting a distant delicate note, which seemed to float and tenderly multiply upon itself--a variation, indeed, of the tune which De Casson had played. A rapt look came into his eyes. And all that look behind the general look of his face--the look which has to do with a man's past or future--deepened and spread, till you saw, for once in a way, a strong soldier turned artist, yet only what was masculine and strong. The music deepened also, and, as the priest opened the door, swept against him like a wind so warm that a moisture came to his eyes. "Iberville!" he said, in a glad voice. "Pierre!"

The violin was down on the instant. "My dear abbe!" he cried. And then the two embraced.

"How do you like my entrance?" said the young man. "But I had to provide my own music!" He laughed, and ran his hands affectionately down the arms of the priest.

"I had been playing the same old chansonette--"

"With your original variations?"

"With my poor variations, just before you came in; and that done--"

"Yes, yes, abbe, I know the rest: prayers for the safe return of the sailor, who for four years or nearly has been learning war in King Louis's ships, and forgetting the good old way of fighting by land, at which he once served his prentice time--with your blessing, my old tutor, my good fighting abbe! Do you remember when we stopped those Dutchmen on the Richelieu, and you--"

The priest interrupted with a laugh. "But, my dear Iberville--"

"It was 'Pierre' a minute gone; 'twill be 'Monsieur Pierre le Moyne of Iberville' next," the other said in mock reproach, as he went to the fire.

"No, no; I merely--"

"I understand. Pardon the wild youth who plagues his old friend and teacher, as he did long ago--so much has happened since."

His face became grave and a look of trouble came. Presently the priest said: "I never had a pupil whose teasing was so pleasant, poor humourist that I am. But now, Pierre, tell me all, while I lay out what the pantry holds."

The gay look came back into Iberville's face. "Ahem," he said--"which is the way to begin a wonderful story: Once upon a time a young man, longing to fight for his king by land alone, and with special fighting of his own to do hard by"--(here De Casson looked at him keenly and a singular light came into his eyes)--"was wheedled away upon the king's ships to France, and so

> 'Left the song of the spinning-wheel,
> The hawk and the lady fair,
> And sailed away--'

But the song is old and so is the story, abbe; so here's the brief note of it. After years of play and work,--play in France and stout work in the Spaniards' country,--he was shipped away to

> 'Those battle heights, Quebec heights, our own heights,
> The citadel our golden lily bears,
> And Frontenac--'

But I babble again. And at Quebec he finds the old song changed. The heights and the lilies are there, but Frontenac, the great, brave Frontenac, is gone: confusion lives where only conquest and honest quarrelling were--"

"Frontenac will return--there is no other way!" interposed De Casson.

"Perhaps. And the young man looked round and lo! old faces and places had changed. Children had grown into women, with children at their breasts; young wives had become matronly; and the middle-aged were slaving servants and apothecaries to make them young again. And the young man turned from the world he used to know, and said: 'There are but three things in the world worth doing--loving, roaming, and fighting.' Therefore, after one day, he turned from the poor little Court-game at Quebec, travelled to Montreal, spent a few hours with his father and his brothers, Bienville, Longueil, Maricourt, and Sainte-Helene, and then, having sent word to his dearest friend, came to see him, and found him -- his voice got softer--the same as of old: ready with music and wine and aves for the prodigal."

He paused. The priest had placed meat and wine on the table, and now he came and put his hand on Iberville's shoulder. "Pierre," he said, "I welcome you as one brother might another, the elder foolishly fond." Then he added: "I was glad you remembered our music."

"My dear De Casson, as if I could forget! I have yet the Maggini you gave me. It was of the things for remembering. If we can't be loyal to our first loves, why to anything?"

"Even so, Pierre; but few at your age arrive at that. Most people learn it when they have bartered away every dream. It is enough to have a few honest emotions--very few--and stand by them till all be done."

"Even hating?" Iberville's eyes were eager.

"There is such a thing as a noble hate."

"How every inch of you is man!" answered the other, clasping the priest's arms. Then he added: "Abbe, you know what I long to hear. You have been to New York twice; you were there within these three months--"

"And was asked to leave within these three months--banished, as it were."

"I know. You said in your letter that you had news. You were kind to go--"

"Perrot went too."

"My faithful Perrot! I was about to ask of him. I had a birch-bark letter from him, and he said he would come--Ah, here he is!"

He listened. There was a man's voice singing near by. They could even hear the words:

"'O the young seigneur! O the young seigneur!
A hundred bucks in a day he slew;
And the lady gave him a ribbon to wear,
And a shred of gold from her golden hair
O the way of a maid was the way he knew;
O the young seigneur! O the young seigneur!'"

"Shall we speak freely before him?" said the priest. "As freely as you will. Perrot is true. He was with me, too, at the beginning."

At that moment there came a knock, and in an instant the coureur du bois had caught the hands of the young man, and was laughing up in his face.

"By the good Sainte Anne, but you make Nick Perrot a dwarf, dear monsieur!"

"Well, well, little man, I'll wager neither the great abbe here nor myself could bring you lower than you stand, for all that. Comrade, 'tis kind of you to come so prompt."

"What is there so good as the face of an old friend!" said Perrot, with a little laugh. "You will drink with a new, and eat with a coming friend, and quarrel with either; but 'tis only the old friend that knows the old trail, and there's nothing to a man like the way he has come in the world."

"The trail of the good comrade," said the priest softly.

"Ah!" responded Perrot, "I remember, abbe, when we were at the Portneuf you made some verses of that--eh! eh! but they were good!"

"No fitter time," said Iberville; "come, abbe, the verses!"

"No, no; another day," answered the priest.

It was an interesting scene. Perrot, short, broad, swarthy, dressed in rude buckskin gaudily ornamented, bandoleer and belt garnished with silver,--a recent gift of some grateful merchant, standing between the powerful black-robed priest and this gallant sailor-soldier, richly dressed in fine skins and furs, with long waving hair, more like a Viking than a man of fashion, and carrying a courtly and yet sportive look, as though he could laugh at the miseries of the sinful world. Three strange comrades were these, who knew each other so far as one man can know another, yet each knowing from a different stand-point. Perrot knew certain traits of Iberville of which De Casson was ignorant, and the abbe knew many depths which Perrot never even vaguely plumbed. And yet all could meet and be free in speech, as though each read the other thoroughly.

"Let us begin," said Iberville. "I want news of New York."

"Let us eat as we talk," urged the abbe.

They all sat and were soon eating and drinking with great relish.

Presently the abbe began:

"Of my first journey you know by the letter I sent you: how I found that Mademoiselle Leveret was gone to England with her father. That was a year after you left, now about three years gone. Monsieur Gering entered the navy of the English king, and went to England also."

Iberville nodded. "Yes, yes, in the English navy I know very well of that."

The abbe looked up surprised. "From my letter?"

"I saw him once in the Spaniards' country," said Iberville, "when we swore to love each other less and less."

"What was the trouble?" asked the priest.

"Pirates' booty, which he, with a large force, seized as a few of my men were carrying it to the coast. With his own hand he cut down my servant, who had been with me since from the first. Afterwards in a parley I saw him, and we exchanged--compliments. The sordid gentleman thought I was fretting about the booty. Good God, what are some thousand pistoles to the blood of one honest friend!"

"And in your mind another leaven worked," ventured the priest.

"Another leaven, as you say," responded Iberville. "So, for your story, abbe."

"Of the first journey there is nothing more to tell, save that the English governor said you were as brave a gentleman as ever played ambassador-- which was, you remember, much in Count Frontenac's vein."

Iberville nodded and smiled. "Frontenac railed at my impertinence also."

"But gave you a sword when you told him the news of Radisson," inter- jected Perrot. "And by and by I've things to say of him."

The abbe continued: "For my second visit, but a few months ago. We priests have gone much among the Iroquois, even in the English country, and, as I promised you, I went to New York. There I was summoned to the governor. He commanded me to go back to Quebec. I was about to ask him of Mademoiselle when there came a tap at the door The governor looked at me a little sharply. 'You are,' said he, 'a friend of Monsieur Iberville. You shall know one who keeps him in remembrance.' Then he let the lady enter. She had heard that I was there, having seen Perrot first."

Here Perrot, with a chuckle, broke in: "I chanced that way, and I had a wish to see what was for seeing; for here was our good abbe alone among the wolves, and there were Radisson and the immortal Bucklaw, of whom there was news."

De Casson still continued: "When I was presented she took my hand and said: 'Monsieur l'Abbe, I am glad to meet a friend--an old friend--of Monsieur Iberville. I hear that he has been in France and elsewhere.'"

Here the abbe paused, smiling as if in retrospect, and kept looking into the fire and turning about in his hand his cassock-cord.

Iberville had sat very still, his face ruled to quietness; only his eyes showing the great interest he felt. He waited, and presently said: "Yes, and then?"

The abbe withdrew his eyes from the fire and turned them upon Iberville.

"And then," he said, "the governor left the room. When he had gone she came to me, and, laying her hand upon my arm, said: 'Monsieur, I know you are to be trusted. You are the friend of a brave man.'"

The abbe paused, and smiled over at Iberville. "You see," he said, "her trust was in your friend, not in my office. Well, presently she added: 'I know that Monsieur Iberville and Mr. Gering, for a foolish quarrel of years ago, still are cherished foes. I wish your help to make them both happier; for no man can be happy and hate.' And I gave my word to do so." Here Perrot chuckled to himself and interjected softly: "Mon Dieu! she could make a man say anything at all. I would have sworn to her that while I lived I never should fight. Eh, that's so!"

"Allons!" said Iberville impatiently, yet grasping the arm of the woodsman kindly.

The abbe once more went on: "When she had ended questioning I said to her: 'And what message shall I give from you?' 'Tell him,' she answered, 'by the right of lifelong debt I ask for peace.' 'Is that all?' said I. 'Tell him,' she added, 'I hope we may meet again.' 'For whose sake,' said I, 'do you ask for peace?' 'I am a woman,' she answered, 'I am selfish--for my own sake.'"

Again the priest paused, and again Iberville urged him.

"I asked if she had no token. There was a flame in her eye, and she begged me to excuse her. When she came back she handed me a little packet. 'Give it to Monsieur Iberville,' she said, 'for it is his. He lent it to me years ago. No doubt he has forgotten.'"

At that the priest drew from his cassock a tiny packet, and Iberville, taking, opened it. It held a silver buckle tied by a velvet ribbon. A flush crept slowly up Iberville's face from his chin to his hair, then he sighed, and presently, out of all reason, laughed.

"Indeed, yes; it is mine," he said. "I very well remember when I found it."

Here Perrot spoke. "I very well remember, monsieur, when she took it from your doublet; but it was on a slipper then."

Iberville did not answer, but held the buckle, rubbing it on his sleeve as though to brighten it. "So much for the lady," he said at last; "what more?"

"I learned," answered the abbe, "that Monsieur Gering was in Boston, and that he was to go to Fort Albany at Hudson's Bay, where, on our territory, the English have set forts."

Here Perrot spoke. "Do you know, monsieur, who are the poachers? No? Eh? No? Well, it is that Radisson."

Iberville turned sharply upon Perrot. "Are you sure of that?" he said. "Are you sure, Nick?"

"As sure as I've a head. And I will tell you more: Radisson was with Bucklaw at the kidnapping. I had the pleasure to kill a fellow of Bucklaw, and he told me that before he died. He also told how Bucklaw went with Radisson to the Spaniards' country treasure-hunting. Ah! there are many fools in the world. They did not get the treasure. They quarreled, and Radisson went to the far north, Bucklaw to the far south. The treasure is where it was. Eh bien, such is the way of asses."

Iberville was about to speak.

"But wait," said Perrot, with a slow, tantalising smile; "it is not wise to hurry. I have a mind to know; so while I am at New York I go to Boston. It makes a man's mind great to travel. I have been east to Boston; I have been west beyond the Ottawa and the Michilimackinac, out to the Mississippi. Yes. Well, what did I find in Boston? Peste! I found that they were all like men in purgatory--sober and grave. Truly. And so dull! Never a saint-day, never a feast, never a grand council when the wine, the rum, flow so free, and you shall eat till you choke. Nothing. Everything is stupid; they do not smile. And so the Indians make war! Well, I have found this. There is a great man from the Kennebec called William Phips. He has traded in the Indies. Once while he was there he heard of that treasure. Ha! ha! There have been so many fools on that trail. The governor of New York was a fool when Bucklaw played his game; he would have been a greater if he had gone with Bucklaw."

Here Iberville would have spoken, but Perrot waved his hand. "De grace, a minute only. Monsieur Gering, the brave English lieutenant, is at Hudson's Bay, and next summer he will go with the great William Phips-- Tonnerre, what a name--William Phips! Like a pot of herring! He will go with him after the same old treasure. Boston is a big place, but I hear these things."

Usually a man of few words, Perrot had bursts of eloquence, and this was one of them. But having made his speech, he settled back to his tobacco and into the orator's earned repose.

Iberville looked up from the fire and said: "Perrot, you saw her in New York. What speech was there between you?"

Perrot's eyes twinkled. "There was not much said.

"I put myself in her way. When she saw me her cheek came like a peach-blossom. 'A very good morning, ma'm'selle,' said I, in English. She smiled and said the same. 'And your master, where is he?' she asked with a fine smile. 'My friend Monsieur Iberville?' I said; 'ah! he will be in Quebec soon.' Then I told her of the abbe, and she took from a chain a little medallion and gave it me in memory of the time we saved her. And before I could say Thank you, she had gone--Well, that is all --except this."

He drew from his breast a chain of silver, from which hung the gold medallion, and shook his head at it with good-humour. But presently a hard look came on his face, and he was changed from the cheerful woodsman into the chief of bushrangers. Iberville read the look, and presently said:

"Perrot, men have fought for less than gold from a woman's chain and a buckle from her shoe."

"I have fought from Trois Pistoles to Michilimackinac for the toss of a louis-d'or."

"As you say. Well, what think you--"

He paused, rose, walked up and down the room, caught his moustache between his teeth once or twice, and seemed buried in thought. Once or twice he was about to speak, but changed his mind. He was calculating many things: planning, counting chances, marshalling his resources. Presently he glanced round the room. His eyes fell on a map. That was it. It was a mere outline, but enough. Putting his finger on it, he sent it up, up, up, till it settled on the shores of Hudson's Bay. Again he ran the finger from the St. Lawrence up the coast and through Hudson's Straits, but shook his head in negation. Then he stood, looked at the map steadily, and presently, still absorbed, turned to the table. He saw the violin, picked it up, and handed it to De Casson:

"Something with a smack of war," he said. "And a woman for me," added Perrot.

The abbe shook his head musingly at Perrot, took the violin, and gathered it to his chin. At first he played as if in wait of something that eluded him. But all at once he floated into a powerful melody, as a stream creeps softly through a weir, and after many wanderings broadens suddenly into a great stream. He had found his theme. Its effect was striking. Through Iberville's mind there ran a hundred incidents of his life, one chasing upon the other without sequence--phantasmagoria out of the scene--house of memory:

The light upon the arms of De Tracy's soldiers when they marched up Mountain Street many years before--The frozen figure of a man standing upright in the plains--A procession of canoes winding down past Two Mountains, the wild chant of the Indians joining with the romantic songs of the voyageurs--A girl flashing upon the drawn swords of two lads--King Louis giving his hand to one of these lads to kiss--A lady of the Court for whom he might easily have torn his soul to rags, but for a fair-faced English girl, ever like a delicate medallion in his eye--A fight with the English in the Spaniards' country--His father blessing him as he went forth to France--A dark figure taking a hundred shapes, and yet always meaning the same as when he--Iberville--said over the governor's table in New York, "Foolish boy!"--A vast stretch of lonely forest, in the white coverlet of winter, through which sounded now and then the boom-boom of a bursting tree-- A few score men upon a desolate northern track, silent, desperate, courageous; a forlorn hope on the edge of the Arctic circle, with the joy of conquest in their bones, and at their thighs the swords of men.

These are a few of the pictures, but the last of them had not to do with the past: a dream grown into a fact, shaped by the music, become at once an emotion and a purpose.

Iberville had now driven home the first tent-peg of a wonderful adventure. Under the spell of that music his body seemed to grow larger. He fingered his sword, and presently caught Perrot by the shoulder and said "We will do it, Perrot."

Perrot got to his feet. He understood. He nodded and seized Iberville's hand. "Bravo! There was nothing else to do," he replied.

De Casson lowered his violin. "What do you intend?" he asked gravely.

Iberville took his great hand and pressed it. "To do what you will commend, abbe: at Hudson's Bay to win back forts the English have taken, and get those they have built."

"You have another purpose," added De Casson softly.

"Abbe, that is between me and my conscience. I go for my king and country against our foes."

"Who will go with you? You will lead?"

"Not I to lead--that involves me." Iberville's face darkened. "I wish more freedom, but still to lead in fact."

"But who will lead? And who will go?"

"De Troyes, perhaps, to lead. To go, my brothers Sainte-Helene and Maricourt, Perrot and a stout company of his men; and then I fear not treble as many English."

The priest did not seem satisfied. Presently Iberville, with a winning smile, ran an arm over his shoulder and added: "We cannot go without you, Dollier."

The priest's face cleared, and a moment afterwards the three comrades shook hands together.

AS SEEN THROUGH A GLASS, DARKLY

WHEN King Louis and King James called for peace, they could not know that it was as little possible to their two colonies as between rival buccaneers. New France was full of bold spirits who loved conquest for conquest's sake. Besides, in this case there was a force at work, generally unknown, but as powerful as the convincing influence of an army. Behind the worst and the best acts of Charles II was a woman. Behind the glories and follies of Louis XIV was also a woman. Behind some of the most striking incidents in the history of New France, New England, and New York, was a woman.

We saw her when she was but a child--the centre of singular events. Years had passed. Not one of those events had gone for nothing; each was bearing fruit after its kind.

She is sitting alone in a room of a large unhandsome house, facing on Boston harbour. It is evening. The room itself is of dark wood, and evening has thrown it into gloom. Yet somehow the girl's face has a light of its own. She is turned fair towards the window, and is looking out to sea. A mist is rising from the water, and the shore is growing grey and heavy as the light in the west recedes and night creeps in from the ocean. She watches the waves and the mist till all is mist without; a scene which she had watched, how often she could not count. The night closes in entirely upon her, but she does not move. At last the door of the room opens and some one enters and closes it again. "My daughter!" says an anxious voice. "Are you here, Jessica?"

"I am here, father," is the reply. "Shall we have lights?"

"As you will."

Even as they speak a servant enters, and lighted candles are put upon the table. They are alone again. Both are pale. The girl stands very still, and so quiet is her face, one could never guess that she is passing, through the tragic moment of her life.

"What is your answer, Jessica?" he asks. "I will marry him when he comes back."

"Thank God!" is the old man's acknowledgment. "You have saved our fortunes."

The girl sighs, and then, with a little touch of that demure irony which we had seen in her years before, says: "I trust we have not lost our honour."

"Why, you love him, do you not? There is no one you care for more than George Gering?"

"I suppose not," is her reply, but the tone is enigmatical.

While this scene is on, another appears in Cheapside, London. A man of bold and vigorous bearing comes from the office of a well-known solicitor. That very morning he had had an interview with the King, and had been reminded with more exactness than kindness that he had cost King Charles a ship, scores of men, and thousands of pounds, in a fruitless search for buried treasure in Hispaniola. When he had urged his case upon the basis of fresh information, he was drily told that the security was too scant, even for a king. He had then pleaded his case to the Duke of Albemarle and other distinguished gentlemen. They were seemingly convinced, but withheld their answer till the following morning.

But William Phips, stubborn adventurer, destined to receive all sorts of honours in his time, has no intention of quitting London till he has his way; and this is his thought as he steps into Cheapside, having already made preparations upon the chance of success. He has gone so far as to purchase a ship, called the Bridgwater Merchant from an alderman in London, though he has not a hundred guineas at his disposal. As he stands debating, a hand touches his arm and a voice says in his ear: "You were within a mile of it with the Atgier Rose, two years ago."

The great adventurer turns. "The devil I was! And who are you?"

Satanic humour plays in the stranger's eyes as he answers: "I am Edward Bucklaw, pirate and keeper of the treasure-house in the La Planta River."

"Blood of Judas," Phips says, "how dare you speak to me? I'll have you in yon prison for an unhung rascal!"

"Ah! you are a great man," is the unmoved reply. "I knew you'd feel that way. But if you'll listen for five minutes, down here at the Bull-and-Daisy, there shall be peace between us."

An hour later, Phips, following Bucklaw's instructions, is tracing on a map the true location of the lost galleon's treasure.

"Then," says Bucklaw, "we are comrades?"

"We are adventurers."

Another scene. In a northern inland sea two men are standing on the deck of a ship: the one stalwart, clear-eyed, with a touch of strong reserve in face and manner; the other of middle height, with sinister look. The former is looking out silently upon the great locked hummocks of ice surrounding the vessel. It is the early morning. The sun is shining with that hard brightness only seen in the Arctic world--keen as silver, cold as steel. It plays upon the hummocks, and they send out shafts of light at fantastic angles, and a thin blue line runs between the almost unbearable general radiance and the sea of ice stretching indefinitely away. But to the west is a shore, and on it stands a fort and a few detached houses. Upon the walls of the fort are some guns, and the British flag is flying above. Beyond these again are the plains of the north--the home of the elk, musk-ox, silver fox, the white bear and the lonely races of the Pole. Here and there, in the south-west, an island of pines breaks the monotony, but to the north there is only the white silence, the terrible and yet beautiful trail of the Arctic.

The smaller man stands swinging his arms for warmth; the smack of the leather in the clear air like the report of a gun. Presently, stopping his exercise, he says:

"Well, monsieur, what do you say?"

Slowly the young man withdraws his eyes from the scene and turns.

"Radisson," he says, "this is much the same story as Bucklaw told Governor Nicholls. How come you to know of it?"

"You remember, I was proclaimed four years ago? Well, afterwards I fell in with Bucklaw. I sailed with him to the Spaniards' country, and we might have got the treasure, but we quarreled; there was a fight, and I--well, we end. Bucklaw was captured by the French and was carried to France. He was a fool to look for the treasure with a poor ship and a worse crew. He was for getting William Phips, a man of Boston, to work with him, for Phips had got something of the secret from an old sailor, but when he would have got him, Phips was on his way with a ship of King Charles. I will tell you something more.' Mademoiselle Leveret's--"

"What do you know of Mademoiselle Leveret?"

"A little. Mademoiselle's father lost much money in Phips's expedition."

"How know you that?"

"I have ears. You have promised to go with Phips. Isn't that so?"

"What then?"

"I will go with you."

"Booty?"

"No, revenge."

"On whom?"

"The man you hate--Iberville."

Gering's face darkens. "We are not likely to meet."

"Pardon! very likely. Six months ago he was coming back from France. He will find you. I know the race."

A sneer is on Gering's face. "Freebooters, outlaws like yourself!"

"Pardon! gentlemen, monsieur; noble outlaws. What is it that once or twice they have quarreled with the governor, and because they would not yield have been proclaimed? Nothing. Proclaimed yesterday, today at Court. No, no. I hate Iberville, but he is a great man."

In the veins of the renegade is still latent the pride of race. He is a villain but he knows the height from which he fell. "He will find you, monsieur," he repeats. "When Le Moyne is the hunter he never will kennel till the end. Besides, there is the lady!"

"Silence!"

Radisson knows that he has said too much. His manner changes. "You will let me go with you?" The Englishman remembers that this scoundrel was with Bucklaw, although he does not know that Radisson was one of the abductors.

"Never!" he says, and turns upon his heel.

A moment after and the two have disappeared from the lonely pageant of ice and sun. Man has disappeared, but his works--houses and ships and walls and snow-topped cannon--lie there in the hard grasp of the North, while the White Weaver, at the summit of the world, is shuttling these lives into the woof of battle, murder, and sudden death.

On the shore of the La Planta River a man lies looking into the sunset. So sweet, so beautiful is the landscape, the deep foliage, the scent of flowers, the flutter of bright-winged birds, the fern-grown walls of a ruined town, the wallowing eloquence of the river, the sonorous din of the locust, that none could think this a couch of death. A Spanish priest is making ready for that last long voyage, when the soul of man sloughs the dross of earth. Beside him kneels another priest--a Frenchman of the same order.

The dying man feebly takes from his breast a packet and hands it to his friend.

"It is as I have said," he whispers. "Others may guess, but I know. I know--and another. The rest are all dead. There were six of us, and all were killed save myself. We were poisoned by a Spaniard. He thought he had killed all, but I lived. He also was killed. His murderer's name was Bucklaw--an English pirate. He has the secret. Once he came with a ship to find, but there was trouble and he did not go on. An Englishman also came with the king's ship, but he did not find. But I know that the man Bucklaw will come again. It should not be. Listen: A year ago, and something more, I was travelling to the coast. From there I was to sail for Spain. I had lost the chart of the river then. I was taken ill and I should have died, but a young French officer stayed his men beside me and cared for me, and had me carried to the coast, where I recovered. I did not go to Spain, and I found the chart of the river again."

There is a pause, in which the deep breathing of the dying man mingles with the low wash of the river, and presently he speaks again. "I vowed then that he should know. As God is our Father, swear that you will give this packet to himself only."

The priest, in reply, lifts the crucifix from the dying man's breast and puts his lips to it. The world seems not to know, so cheerful is it all, that, with a sob, that sob of farewell which the soul gives the body,-- the spirit of a man is passing the mile-posts called Life, Time, and Eternity.

Yet another glance into passing incidents before we follow the straight trail of our story. In the city of Montreal fourscore men are kneeling in a little church, as the mass is slowly chanted at the altar. All of them are armed. By the flare of the torches and the candles--for it is not daybreak yet--you can see the flash of a scabbard, the glint of a knife, and the sheen of a bandoleer.

Presently, from among them, one man rises, goes to the steps of the sanctuary and kneels. He is the leader of the expedition, the Chevalier de Troyes, the chosen of the governor. A moment, and three other men rise and come and kneel beside him. These are three brothers, and one we know--gallant, imperious, cordial, having the superior ease of the courtier.

The four receive a blessing from a massive, handsome priest, whose face, as it bends over Iberville, suddenly flushes with feeling. Presently the others rise, but Iberville remains an instant longer, as if loth to leave. The priest whispers to him: "Be strong, be just, be merciful."

The young man lifts his eyes to the priest's: "I will be just, abbe!"

Then the priest makes the sacred gesture over him.

TO THE PORCH OF THE WORLD

THE English colonies never had a race of woodsmen like the coureurs du bois of New France. These were a strange mixture: French peasants, half-breeds, Canadian-born Frenchmen, gentlemen of birth with lives and fortunes gone askew, and many of the native Canadian noblesse, who, like the nobles of France, forbidden to become merchants, became adventurers with the coureurs du bois, who were ever with them in spirit more than with the merchant. The peasant prefers the gentleman to the bourgeois as his companion. Many a coureur du bois divided his tale of furs with a distressed noble or seigneur, who dare not work in the fields.

The veteran Charles le Moyne, with his sons, each of whom played a daring and important part in the history of New France,--Iberville greatest,-- was one of the few merchants in whom was combined the trader and the noble. But he was a trader by profession before he became a seigneur. In his veins was a strain of noble blood; but leaving France and settling in Canada, he avoided the little Court at Quebec, went to Montreal, and there began to lay the foundation of his fame and fortune, and to send forth men who were as the sons of Jacob. In his heart he was always in sympathy with the woodsmen, and when they were proclaimed as perilous to the peace and prosperity of the king's empire, he stood stoutly by them. Adventurers, they traded as they listed; and when the Intendant Duchesnau could not bend them to his greedy will, they were to be caught and hanged wherever found. King Louis hardly guessed that to carry out that order would be to reduce greatly the list of his Canadian noblesse. It struck a blow at the men who, in one of the letters which the grim Frontenac sent to Versailles not long before his death, were rightly called "The King's Traders"--more truly such than any others in New France.

Whether or not the old seigneur knew it at the time, three of his own sons were among the coureurs du bois--chieftains by courtesy--when they were proclaimed. And it was like Iberville, that, then only a lad, he came in from the woods, went to his father, and astonished him by asking for his blessing. Then he started for Quebec, and arriving there with Perrot and Du Lhut, went to the citadel at night and asked to be admitted to Count

Frontenac. Perhaps the governor-grand half-barbarian as he was at heart-guessed the nature of the visit and, before he admitted Iberville, dismissed those who were with him. There is in an old letter still preserved by an ancient family of France, an account of this interview, told by a cynical young nobleman. Iberville alone was admitted. His excellency greeted his young visitor courteously, yet with hauteur.

"You bring strange comrades to visit your governor, Monsieur Iberville," he said.

"Comrades in peace, your excellency, comrades in war."

"What war?"

"The king makes war against the coureurs du bois. There is a price on the heads of Perrot and Du Lhut. We are all in the same boat."

"You speak in riddles, sir."

"I speak of riddles. Perrot and Du Lhut are good friends of the king. They have helped your excellency with the Indians a hundred times. Their men have been a little roystering, but that's no sin. I am one with them, and I am as good a subject as the king has."

"Why have you come here?"

"To give myself up. If you shoot Perrot or Du Lhut you will have to shoot me; and, if you carry on the matter, your excellency will not have enough gentlemen to play Tartufe."

This last remark referred to a quarrel which Frontenac had had with the bishop, who inveighed against the governor's intention of producing Tartufe at the chateau.

Iberville's daring was quite as remarkable as the position in which he had placed himself. With a lesser man than Frontenac it might have ended badly. But himself, courtier as he was, had ever used heroical methods, and appreciated the reckless courage of youth. With grim humour he put all three under arrest, made them sup with him, and sent them away secretly before morning--free. Before Iberville left, the governor had word with him alone.

"Monsieur," he said, "you have a keen tongue, but our king needs keen swords, and since you have the advantage of me in this, I shall take care you pay the bill. We have had enough of outlawry. You shall fight by rule and measure soon."

"In your excellency's bodyguard, I hope," was the instant reply.

"In the king's navy," answered Frontenac, with a smile, for he was pleased with the frank flattery.

A career different from that of George Gering, who, brought up with Puritans, had early learned to take life seriously, had little of Iberville's gay spirit, but was just such a determined, self-conscious Englishman as any one could trust and admire, and none but an Englishman love.

And Jessica Leveret? Wherever she had been during the past four years, she had stood between these two men, regardful, wondering, waiting; and at last, as we know, casting the die against the enemy of her country. But was it cast after all?

Immediately after she made a certain solemn promise, recorded in the last chapter, she went once again to New York to visit Governor Nicholls. She had been there some months before, but it was only for a few weeks, and then she had met Dollier de Casson and Perrot. That her mind was influenced by memory of Iberville we may guess, but in what fashion who can say? It is not in mortal man to resolve the fancies of a woman, or interpret the shadowy inclinations, the timid revulsions, which move them--they cannot tell why, any more than we. They would indeed be thankful to be solved unto themselves. The great moment for a man with a woman is when, by some clear guess or some special providence, he shows her in a flash her own mind. Her respect, her serious wonder, are all then making for his glory. Wise and happy if by a further touch of genius he seizes the situation: henceforth he is her master. George Gering and Jessica had been children together, and he understood her, perhaps, as, did no one else, save her father; though he never made good use of his knowledge, nor did he touch that side of her which was purely feminine--her sweet inconsis-tency; therefore, he was not her master.

But he had appealed to her, for he had courage, strong, ambition, thorough kindness, and fine character, only marred by a want of temperament. She had avoided as long as she could the question which, on his return from service in the navy, he asked her, almost without warning; and with a touch of her old demureness and gaiety she had put him off, bidding him go win his laurels as commander. He was then commissioned for Hudson's Bay, and expected, on his return, to proceed to the Spaniards' country with William Phips, if that brave gentleman succeeded with the king or his nobles. He had gone north with his ship, and, as we have seen, when Iberville started on that almost impossible journey, was preparing to return to Boston. As he waited Iberville came on.

QUI VIVE!

FROM Land's End to John O' Groat's is a long tramp, but that from Montreal to Hudson's Bay is far longer, and yet many have made it; more, however, in the days of which we are writing than now, and with greater hardships also then. But weighed against the greater hardships there was a bolder temper and a more romantic spirit.

How strange and severe a journey it was, only those can tell who have travelled those wastes, even in these later days, when paths have been beaten down from Mount Royal to the lodges of the North. When they started, the ice had not yet all left the Ottawa River, and they wound their way through crowding floes, or portaged here and there for miles, the eager sun of spring above with scarcely a cloud to trail behind him. At last the river cleared, and for leagues they travelled to the north-west, and came at last to the Lake of the Winds. They travelled across one corner of it, to a point where they would strike an unknown path to Hudson's Bay.

Iberville had never before seen this lake, and, with all his knowledge of great proportions, he was not prepared for its splendid vastness. They came upon it in the evening, and camped beside it. They watched the sun spread out his banners, presently veil his head in them, and sink below the world. And between them and that sunset was a vast rock stretching out from a ponderous shore--a colossal stone lion, resting Sphinxlike, keeping its faith with the ages. Alone, the warder of the West, stormy, menacing, even the vernal sun could give it little cheerfulness. But to Iberville and his followers it brought no gloom at night, nor yet in the morning when all was changed, and a soft silver mist hung over the "great water," like dissolving dew, through which the sunlight came with a strange, solemn delicacy. Upon the shore were bustle, cheerfulness, and song, until every canoe was launched, and then the band of warriors got in, and presently were away in the haze.

The long bark canoes, with lofty prows, stained with powerful dyes, slid along this path swiftly, the paddles noiselessly cleaving the water with the precision of a pendulum. One followed the other with a space between, so that Iberville, in the first, looking back, could see a diminishing procession, the last seeming large and weird--almost a shadow--as it were a part of the weird atmosphere. On either side was that soft plumbless diffusion, and ahead the secret of untravelled wilds and the fortunes of war.

As if by common instinct, all gossip ceased soon after they left the shore, and, cheerful as was the French Canadian, he was--and is-- superstitious. He saw sermons in stones, books in the running brooks, and the supernatural in everything. Simple, hardy, occasionally bloody, he was ever on the watch for signs and wonders, and a phase of nature influenced him after the manner of a being with a temperament. Often, as some of the woodsmen and river-men had seen this strange effect, they now made the sacred gesture as they ran on. The pure moisture lay like a fine exudation on their brown skins, glistened on their black hair, and hung from their beards, giving them a mysterious look. The colours of their canoes and clothes were softened by the dim air and long use, and there seemed to accompany each boat and each person an atmosphere within this other haze, a spiritual kind of exhalation; so that one might have thought them, with the crucifixes on their breasts, and that unworldly, distinguished look which comes to those who live much with nature, as sons of men going upon such mission as did they who went into the far land with Arthur.

But the silence could not be maintained for long. The first flush of the impression gone, these half-barbarians, with the simple hearts of children, must rise from the almost melancholy, somewhat religious mood, into which they had been cast. As Iberville, with Sainte-Helene and Perrot, sat watching the canoes that followed, with voyageurs erect in bow and stern, a voice in the next canoe, with a half-chanting modulation, began a song of the wild-life. Voice after voice slowly took it up, until it ran along the whole procession. A verse was sung, then a chorus altogether, then a refrain of one verse which was sung by each boat in succession to the last. As the refrain of this was sung by the last boat it seemed to come out of the great haze behind. Verses of the old song are still preserved:

> "Qui vive!
> Who is it cries in the dawn
> Cries when the stars go down?
> Who is it comes through the mist
> The mist that is fine like lawn,
> The mist like an angel's gown?

Who is it comes in the dawn?
Qui vive! Qui vive! in the dawn.

"Qui rive!
Who is it passeth us by,
Still in the dawn and the mist?
Tall seigneur of the dawn:
A two-edged sword at his thigh,
A shield of gold at his wrist:
Who is it hurrieth by?
Qui vive! Qui vive! in the dawn."

Under the influence of this beautiful mystery of the dawn, the slow thrilling song, and the strange, happy loneliness--as though they were in the wash between two worlds, Iberville got the great inspiration of his life. He would be a discoverer, the faithful captain of his king, a trader in provinces. . . . And in that he kept his word--years after, but he kept it. There came with this, what always comes to a man of great ideas: the woman who should share his prowess. Such a man, if forced to choose between the woman and the idea, will ever decide for the woman after he has married her, sacrificing what--however much he hides it--lies behind all. But he alone knows what he has sacrificed. For it is in the order of things that the great man shall be first the maker of kingdoms and homes, and then the husband of his wife and a begetter of children. Iberville knew that this woman was not more to him than the feeling just come to him, but he knew also that while the one remained the other would also.

He stood up and folded his arms, looking into the silence and mist. His hand mechanically dropped to his sword, and he glanced up proudly to the silver flag with its golden lilies floating softly on the slight breeze they made as they passed.

"The sword!" he said under his breath. "The world and a woman by the sword; there is no other way."

He had the spirit of his time. The sword was its faith, its magic. If two men loved a woman, the natural way to make happiness for all was to let the sword do its eager office. For they had one of the least-believed and most unpopular of truths, that a woman's love is more a matter of mastery and possession than instinct, two men being of comparatively equal merit and sincerity.

His figure seemed to grow larger in the mist, and the grey haze gave his hair a frosty coating, so that age and youth seemed strangely mingled in him. He stood motionless for a long time as the song went on:

> "Qui vive!
> Who saileth into the morn,
> Out of the wind of the dawn?
> 'Follow, oh, follow me on!'
> Calleth a distant horn.
> He is here--he is there--he is gone,
> Tall seigneur of the dawn!
> Qui vive! Qui vive! in the dawn."

Some one touched Iberville's arm. It was Dollier de Casson. Iberville turned to him, but they did not speak at first--the priest knew his friend well.

"We shall succeed, abbe," Iberville said.

"May our quarrel be a just one, Pierre," was the grave reply.

"The forts are our king's; the man is with my conscience, my dear friend."

"But if you make sorrow for the woman?"

"You brought me a gift from her!" His finger touched his doublet.

"She is English, my Pierre."

"She is what God made her."

"She may be sworn to the man."

Iberville started, then shook his head incredulously. "He is not worthy of her."

"Are you?"

"I know her value better and prize it more."

"You have not seen her for four years."

"I had not seen you for four years--and yet!"

"You saw her then only for a few days--and she was so young!"

"What are days or years? Things lie deep in us till some great moment, and then they spring into life and are ours for ever. When I kissed King Louis' hand I knew that I loved my king; when De Montespan's. I hated, and shall hate always. When I first saw this English girl I waked from youth, I was born again into the world. I had no doubts, I have none now."

"And the man?"

"One knows one's enemy even as the other. There is no way but this, Dollier. He is the enemy of my king, and he is greatly in my debt. Remember the Spaniards' country!"

He laid a hand upon his sword. The face of the priest was calm and grave, but in his eyes was a deep fire. At heart he was a soldier, a loyalist, a gentleman of France. Perhaps there came to him then the dreams of his youth, before a thing happened which made him at last a servant of the Church after he had been a soldier of the king.

Presently the song of the voyageurs grew less, the refrain softened and passed down the long line, and, as it were, from out of far mists came the muffled challenge:

"Qui vive! Qui vive! in the dawn."

Then a silence fell once more. But presently from out of the mists there came, as it were, the echo of their challenge:

"Qui vive! Qui vive! in the dawn."

The paddles stilled in the water and a thrill ran through the line of voyageurs--even Iberville and his friends were touched by it.

Then there suddenly emerged from the haze on their left, ahead of them, a long canoe with tall figures in bow and stern, using paddles. They wore long cloaks, and feathers waved from their heads. In the centre of the canoe was what seemed a body under a pall, at its head and feet small censers. The smell of the wood came to them, and a little trail of sweet smoke was left behind as the canoe swiftly passed into the mist on the other side and was gone.

It had been seen vaguely. No one spoke, no one challenged; it had come and gone like a dream. What it was, no one, not even Iberville, could guess, though he thought it a pilgrimage of burial, such as was sometimes made by distinguished members of Indian tribes. Or it may have been-- which is likely--a dead priest being carried south by Indian friends.

The impression left upon the party was, however, characteristic. There was none but, with the smell of the censers in his nostrils, made the sacred gesture; and had the Jesuit Silvy or the Abbe de Casson been so disposed, the event might have been made into the supernatural.

After a time the mist cleared away, and nothing could be seen on the path they had travelled but the plain of clear water and the distant shore they had left.

Ahead of them was another shore, and they reached this at last. Where the mysterious canoe had vanished, none could tell.

Days upon days, they travelled with incredible labour, now portaging over a stubborn country, now, placing their lives in hazard as they shot down untravelled rapids.

One day on the Black Wing River a canoe was torn open and its three occupants were thrown into the rapids. Two of them were expert swimmers and were able to catch the stern of another canoe as it ran by, and reached safe water, bruised but alive. The third was a boy, Maurice Joval, the youngest of the party, whom Iberville had been at first loth to bring with him. But he had remembered his own ambitious youth, and had consented, persuading De Troyes that the lad was worth encouragement. His canoe was not far behind when the other ran on the rocks. He saw the lad struggle bravely and strike out, but a cross current caught him and carried him towards the steep shore. There he was thrown against a rock.

His strength seemed to fail, but he grasped the rock. It was scraggy, and though it tore and bruised him he clung to it.

Iberville threw off his doublet, and prepared to spring as his boat came down. But another had made ready. It was the abbe, with his cassock gone, and his huge form showing finely. He laid his hand upon Iberville's arm. "Stay here," he said, "I go; I am the stronger."

But Iberville, as cries of warning and appeal rang out around him, the drowning lad had not cried out at all,--sprang into the water. Not alone. The abbe looked around him, made the sacred gesture, and then sprang also into an eddy a distance below, and at an angle made his way up towards the two. Priest though he was, he was also an expert river-man, and his vast strength served him royally. He saw Iberville tossed here and there, but with impossible strength and good fortune reach the lad. The two grasped each other and then struck out for the high shore. De Casson seemed to know what would happen. He altered his course, and, making for the shore also at a point below, reached it. He saw with a kind of despair that it was steep and had no trees; yet his keen eyes also saw, not far below, the dwarfed bole of a tree jutting out from the rock. There lay the chance. Below this was a great turmoil of rapids. A prayer mechanically passed the priest's lips, though his thoughts were those of a warrior then. He almost enjoyed the danger for himself: his fear was for Iberville and for the motherless boy.

He had guessed and hoped aright. Iberville, supporting the now senseless boy, swung down the mad torrent, his eyes blinded with blood so that he could not see. But he heard De Casson's voice, and with a splendid effort threw himself and the lad towards it. The priest also fought upwards to them and caught them as they came, having reserved his great strength until now. Throwing his left arm over the lad he relieved Iberville of his burden, but called to him to hold on. The blood was flowing into Iberville's eyes and he could do nothing else. But now came the fight between the priest and the mad waters. Once--twice--thrice they went beneath, but neither Iberville nor himself let go, and to the apprehensive cries of their friends there succeeded calls of delight, for De Casson had seized the jutting bole and held on. It did not give, and they were safe for a moment.

A quarter of a mile below there was smoother water, and soon the canoes were ashore, and Perrot, Sainte-Helene, and others were running to the rescue. They arrived just in time. Ropes were let down, and the lad was drawn up insensible. Then came the priest, for Iberville, battered as he was, would not stir until the abbe had gone up--a stout strain on the rope. Fortunately there were clefts and fissures in the wall, which could be used in the ascent. De Casson had consented to go first, chiefly because he wished to gratify the still youthful pride of Iberville, who thought the soldier should see the priest into safety. Iberville himself came up slowly, for he was stiff and his limbs were shaking. His clothes were in tatters, and his fine face was like that of a warrior defaced by swords.

But he refused to be carried, and his first care was for the boy, who had received no mortal injury.

"You have saved the boy, Pierre," said the priest, in a low voice.

"Self-abasing always, dear abbe; you saved us both. By heaven, but the king lost a great man in you!"

"Hush! Mere brawn, Pierre. . . . By the blessing of God," he added quickly.

WITH THE STRANGE PEOPLE

AFTER this came varying days of hardship by land and water, and then another danger. One day they were, crossing a great northern lake. The land was moist with the sweat of quick-springing verdure; flocks of wild fowl rose at all points, and herds of caribou came drinking and feeding at the shore. The cries of herons, loons, and river-hens rose with strange distinctness, so delicate was the atmosphere, and the blue of the sky was exquisite.

As they paddled slowly along this lake, keeping time to their songs with the paddles, there suddenly grew out of the distance a great flotilla of canoes with tall prows, and behind them a range of islands which they had not before seen. The canoes were filled with men--Indians, it would seem, by the tall feathers lifting from their heads. A moment before there had been nothing. The sudden appearance was even more startling than the strange canoe that crossed their track on Lake of the Winds. Iberville knew at once that it was a mirage, and the mystery of it did not last long even among the superstitious. But they knew now that somewhere in the north-- presumably not far away--was a large band of Indians, possibly hostile; their own numbers were about fourscore. There was the chance that the Indians were following or intercepting them. Yet, since they had left the Ottawa River, they had seen no human being, save in that strange canoe on Lake of the Winds. To the east were the dreary wastes of Labrador, to the west were the desolate plains and hills, stretching to the valley of the Saskatchewan.

Practically in command, Iberville advised watchfulness and preparation for attack. Presently the mirage faded away as suddenly as it came. For days again they marched and voyaged on, seeing still no human being. At last they came to a lake, which they crossed in their canoes; then they entered the mouth of a small river, travelling northward. The river narrowed at a short distance from its mouth, and at a certain point the stream turned sharply. As the first canoe rounded the point it came full upon half a hundred canoes blocking the river, filled by Indians with bended bows. They were a northern tribe that had never before seen the white man. Tall and stern, they were stout enemies, but they had no firearms, and, as could be seen, they were astonished at the look of the little band, which, at the command of De Troyes, who with Iberville was in the first boat, came steadily on. Suddenly brought face to face there was a pause, in which Iberville, who knew several Indian languages, called to them to make way.

He was not understood, but he had pointed to the white standard of France flaring with the golden lilies; and perhaps the drawn swords and the martial manner of the little band--who had donned gay trappings, it being Iberville's birthday--conveyed in some way his meaning. The bows of the strangers stayed drawn, awaiting word from the leader. Near the chief stood a man seven feet in height, a kind of bodyguard, who presently said something in his ear. He frowned, then seemed to debate, and his face cleared at last. Raising a spear, he saluted the French leaders, and then pointed towards the shore, where there was a space clear of trees, a kind of plateau. De Troyes and Iberville, thinking that a truce and parley were meant, returned the salute with their swords, and presently the canoes of both parties made over to the shore. It was a striking sight: the grave, watchful faces of the Indians, who showed up grandly in the sun, their skin like fine rippling bronze as they moved; their tall feathers tossing, rude bracelets on their wrists, while some wore necklets of brass or copper. The chief was a stalwart savage with a cruel eye, but the most striking figure of all--either French or Indian --was that of the chief's body guard. He was, indeed, the Goliath of the tribe, who, after the manner of other champions, was ever ready for challenge in the name of his master. He was massively built, with long sinewy arms; but Iberville noticed that he was not powerful at the waist in proportion to the rest of his body, and that his neck was thinner than it should be. But these were items, for in all he was a fine piece of humanity, and Iberville said as much to De Casson, involuntarily stretching up as he did so. Tall and athletic himself, he never saw a man of calibre but he felt a wish to measure strength with him, not from vanity, but through the mere instincts of the warrior. Priest as he was, it is possible that De Casson shared the young man's feeling, though chastening years had overcome impulses of youth. It was impossible for the French leaders to guess how this strange parley would end, and when many more Indians suddenly showed on the banks they saw that they might have tough work.

"What do you think of it, Iberville?" said De Troyes. "A juggler's puzzle--let us ask Perrot," was the reply.

Perrot confessed that he knew nothing of this tribe of Indians. The French leaders, who had never heard of Indians who would fight in the open, were, in spite of great opposing numbers, in warrior mood. Presently all the canoes were got to land, and without any hostile sign the Indians filed out on the centre of the plateau, where were pitched a number of tents. The tents were in a circle, surrounding a clear space of ground, and the chief halted in the middle of this. He and his men had scarcely noticed the Frenchmen as they followed, seemingly trusting the honour of the invaders that they would not attack from behind. It was these Indians who had been seen in the mirage. They had followed the Frenchmen, had gone parallel with them for scores of miles, and had at last at this strategic point waylaid them.

The conference was short. The French ranged in column on one side, the Indians on the other, and then the chief stepped forward. De Troyes did the same and not far behind him were Iberville, the other officers, and Perrot. Behind the chief was the champion, then, a little distance away, on either side, the Indian councillors.

The chief waved his hand proudly towards the armed warriors behind him, as if showing their strength, speaking meanwhile, and then with effective gesture, remarking the handful of French. Presently, pointing to his fighting man, he seemed to ask that the matter be settled by single combat.

The French leaders understood: Goliath would have his David. The champion suddenly began a sing-song challenge, during which Iberville and his comrades conferred. The champion's eyes ran up and down the line and alighted on the large form of De Casson, who calmly watched him. Iberville saw this look and could not help but laugh, though the matter was serious. He pictured the good abbe fighting for the band. At this the champion began to beat his breast defiantly.

Iberville threw off his coat, and motioned his friends back. Immediately there was protest. They had not known quite what to do, but Perrot had offered to fight the champion, and they, supposing it was to be a fight with weapons, had hastily agreed. It was clear, however, that it was to be a wrestle to the death. Iberville quelled all protests, and they stepped back. There was a final call from the champion, and then he became silent. From the Indians rose one long cry of satisfaction, and then they too stilled, the chief fell back, and the two men stood alone in the centre. Iberville, whose face had become grave, went to De Casson and whispered to him. The abbe gave him his blessing, and then he turned and went back. He waved his hand to his brothers and his friends,--a gay Cavalier-like motion,--then took off all save his small clothes and stood out.

Never was seen, perhaps, a stranger sight: a gentleman of France ranged against a savage wrestler, without weapons, stripped to the waist, to fight like a gladiator. But this was a new land, and Iberville could ever do what another of his name or rank could not. There was only one other man in Canada who could do the same--old Count Frontenac himself, who, dressed in all his Court finery, had danced a war-dance in the torch-light with Iroquois chiefs.

Stripped, Iberville's splendid proportions could be seen at advantage. He was not massively made, but from crown to heel there was perfect muscular proportion. His admirable training and his splendidly nourished body--cared for, as in those days only was the body cared for--promised much, though against so huge a champion. Then, too, Iberville in his boyhood had wrestled with Indians and had learned their tricks. Added to this were methods learned abroad, which might prove useful now. Yet any one looking at the two would have begged the younger man to withdraw. Never was battle shorter. Iberville, too proud to give his enemy one moment of athletic trifling, ran in on him. For a time they were locked, straining terribly, and then the neck of the champion went with a snap and he lay dead in the middle of the green.

The Indians and the French were both so dumfounded that for a moment no one stirred, and Iberville went back and quietly put on his clothes. But presently cries of rage and mourning came from the Indians, and weapons threatened. But the chief waved aggression down, and came forward to the dead man. He looked for a moment, and then as Iberville and De Troyes came near, he gazed at Iberville in wonder, and all at once reached out both hands to him. Iberville took them and shook them heartily.

There was something uncanny in the sudden death of the champion, and Iberville's achievement had conquered these savages, who, after all, loved such deeds, though at the hand of an enemy. And now the whole scene was changed. The French courteously but firmly demanded homage, and got it, as the superior race can get it from the inferior, when events are, even distantly, in their favour; and here were martial display, a band of fearless men, weapons which the savages had never seen before, trumpets, and, most of all, a chief who was his own champion, and who had snapped the neck of their Goliath as one would break a tree-branch.

From the moment Iberville and the chief shook hands they were friends, and after two days, when they parted company, there was no Indian among all this strange tribe but would have followed him anywhere. As it was, he and De Troyes preferred to make the expedition with his handful of men, and so parted with the Indians, after having made gifts to the chief and his people. The most important of these presents was a musket, handled by the chief at first as though it were some deadly engine. The tribe had been greatly astonished at hearing a volley fired by the whole band at once, and at seeing caribou shot before their eyes; but when the chief himself, after divers attempts, shot a caribou, they stood in proper awe. With mutual friendliness they parted. Two weeks later, after great trials, the band emerged on the shores of Hudson's Bay, almost without baggage, and starving.

OUT OF THE NET

THE last two hundred miles of their journey had been made under trying conditions. Accidents had befallen the canoes which carried the food, and the country through which they passed was almost devoid of game. During the last three days they had little or nothing to eat. When, therefore, at night they came suddenly upon the shores of Hudson's Bay, and Fort Hayes lay silent before them, they were ready for desperate enterprises. The high stockade walls with stout bastions and small cannon looked formidable, yet there was no man of them but was better pleased that the odds were against him than with him. Though it was late spring, the night was cold, and all were wet, hungry, and chilled.

Iberville's first glance at the bay and the fort brought disappointment. No vessel lay in the harbour, therefore it was probable Gering was not there. But there were other forts, and this one must be taken meanwhile. The plans were quickly made. Iberville advised a double attack: an improvised battering-ram at the great gate, and a party to climb the stockade wall at another quarter. This climbing-party he would himself lead, accompanied by his brother Sainte-Helene,

Perrot, and a handful of agile woodsmen. He had his choice, and his men were soon gathered round him. A tree was cut down in the woods some distance from the shore, shortened, and brought down, ready for its duty of battering-ram.

The night was beautiful. There was a bright moon, and the sky by some strange trick of atmosphere had taken on a green hue, against which everything stood out with singular distinctness. The air was placid, and through the stillness came the low humming wash of the water to the hard shore. The fort stood on an upland, looking in its solitariness like some lonely prison-house where men went, more to have done with the world than for punishment. Iberville was in that mood wherein men do stubborn deeds--when justice is more with them than mercy, and selfishness than either.

"If you meet the man, Pierre?" De Casson said before the party started.

Iberville laughed softly. "If we meet, may my mind be his, abbe! But he is not here--there is no vessel, you see! Still, there are more forts on the bay." The band knelt down before they started. It was strange to hear in that lonely waste, a handful of men, bent on a deadly task, singing a low chant of penitence--a Kyrie eleison. Afterwards came the benediction upon this buccaneering expedition, behind which was one man's personal enmity, a merchant company's cupidity, and a great nation's lust of conquest! Iberville stole across the shore and up the hill with his handful of men. There was no sound from the fort; all were asleep. No musket-shot welcomed them, no cannon roared on the night; there was no sentry. What should people on the outposts of the world need of sentries, so long as there were walls to keep out wild animals! In a few moments Iberville and his companions were over the wall. Already the attack on the gate had begun, a passage was quickly made, and by the time Iberville had forced open the doors of the blockhouse, his followers making a wild hubbub as of a thousand men, De Troyes and his party were at his heels. Before the weak garrison could make resistance they were in the hands of their enemies, and soon were gathered in the yard--men, women, and children.

Gering was not there. Iberville was told that he was at one of the other forts along the shore: either Fort Rupert on the east, a hundred and twenty miles away, or at Fort Albany, ninety miles to the north and west. Iberville determined to go to Fort Rupert, and with a few followers, embarking in canoes, assembled before it two nights after. A vessel was in the harbour, and his delight was keen. He divided his men, sending Perrot to take the fort, while himself with a small party moved to the attack of the vessel. Gering had delayed a day too long. He had intended leaving the day before, but the arrival of the governor of the company had induced him to remain another day; entertaining his guest at supper, and toasting him in some excellent wine got in Hispaniola. So palatable was it that all drank deeply, and other liquors found their way to the fo'castle. Thus in the dead of night there was no open eye on the Valiant.

The Frenchmen pushed out gently from the shore, paddled noiselessly over to the ship's side, and clambered up. Iberville was the first to step on deck, and he was followed by Perrot and De Casson, who had, against Iberville's will, insisted on coming. Five others came after. Already they could hear the other party at the gate of the fort, and the cries of the besiegers, now in the fortyard, came clearly to them.

The watch of the Valiant, waking suddenly, sprang up and ran forward, making no outcry, dazed but bent on fighting. He came, however, on the point of Perrot's sabre and was cut down. Meanwhile Iberville, hot for mischief, stamped upon the deck. Immediately a number of armed men came bundling up the hatch way. Among these appeared Gering and the governor, who thrust themselves forward with drawn swords and pistols. The first two men who appeared above the hatchway were promptly despatched, and Iberville's sword was falling upon Gering, whom he did not recognise, when De Casson's hand diverted the blow. It caught the shoulder of a man at Gering's side.

"'Tis Monsieur Gering!" said the priest.

"Stop! stop!" cried a voice behind these. "I am the governor. We surrender."

There was nothing else to do: in spite of Gering's show of defiance, though death was above him if he resisted. He was but half-way up.

"It is no use, Mr. Gering," urged the governor; "they have us like sheep in a pen."

"Very well," said Gering suddenly, handing up his, sword and stepping up himself. "To whom do I surrender?"

"To an old acquaintance, monsieur," said Iberville, coming near, "who will cherish you for the king of France."

"Damnation!" cried Gering, and his eyes hungered for his sword again.

"You would not visit me, so I came to look for you; though why, monsieur, you should hide up here in the porch of the world passeth knowledge."

"Monsieur is witty," answered Gering stoutly; "but if he will grant me my sword again and an hour alone with him, I shall ask no greater joy in life."

By this time the governor was on deck, and he interposed.

"I beg, sir," he said to Iberville, "you will see there is no useless slaughter at yon fort; for I guess that your men have their way with it."

"Shall my messenger, in your name, tell your people to give in?"

"By Heaven, no: I hope that they will fight while remains a chance. And be sure, sir, I should not have yielded here, but that I foresaw hopeless slaughter. Nor would I ask your favour there, but that I know you are like to have bloody barbarians with you--and we have women and children!"

"We have no Indians, we are all French," answered Iberville quietly, and sent the messenger away.

At that moment Perrot touched his arm, and pointed to a man whose shoulder was being bandaged. It was Radisson, who had caught Iberville's sword when the abbe diverted it.

"By the mass," said Iberville; "the gift of the saints!" He pricked Radisson with the point of his sword. "Well, Monsieur Renegade, who holds the spring of the trap now? You have some prayers, I hope. And if there is no priest among your English, we'll find you one before you swing next sundown."

Radisson threw up a malignant look, but said nothing; and went on caring for his wound.

"At sunset, remember. You will see to it, Perrot," he added.

"Pardon me, monsieur," said the governor. "This is an officer of our company, duly surrendered."

"Monsieur will know this man is a traitor, and that I have long-standing orders to kill him wherever found. What has monsieur to say for him?" Iberville added, turning to Gering.

"As an officer of the company," was the reply, "he has the rights of a prisoner of war."

"Monsieur, we have met at the same table, and I cannot think you should plead for a traitor. If you will say that the man--"

But here Radisson broke in. "I want no one to speak for me. I hate you all"--he spat at Iberville--"and I will hang when I must, no sooner."

"Not so badly said," Iberville responded. "'Tis a pity, Radisson, you let the devil buy you."

"T'sh! The devil pays good coin, and I'm not hung yet," he sullenly returned.

By this time all the prisoners save Gering, the governor, and Radisson, were secured. Iberville ordered their disposition, and then, having set a guard, went down to deal with the governor for all the forts on the bay. Because the firing had ceased, he knew that the fort had been captured; and, indeed, word soon came to this effect. Iberville then gave orders that the prisoners from the fort should be brought on board next morning, to be carried on to Fort Albany, which was yet for attack. He was ill-content that a hand-to-hand fight with Gering had been prevented.

He was now all courtesy to the governor and Gering, and, offering them their own wine, entertained them with the hardships of their travel up. He gave the governor assurance that the prisoners should be treated well, and no property destroyed. Afterwards, with apologies, he saw them bestowed in a cabin, the door fastened, and a guard set. Presently he went on deck, and giving orders that Radisson should be kept safe on the after-deck, had rations served out. Then, after eating, he drew his cloak over him in the cabin and fell asleep.

Near daybreak a man came swimming along the side of the ship to the small port-hole of a cabin. He paused before it, took from his pocket a nail, and threw it within. There was no response, and he threw another, and again there was no response. Hearing the step of some one on the deck above he drew in close to the side of the ship, diving under the water and lying still. A moment after he reappeared and moved-almost floated-on to another port-hole. He had only one nail left; he threw it in, and Gering's face appeared.

"Hush, monsieur!" Radisson called up. "I have a key which may fit, and a bar of iron. If you get clear, make for this side."

He spoke in a whisper. At that moment he again heard steps above, and dived as before. The watch looked over, having heard a slight noise; but not knowing that Gering's cabin was beneath, thought no harm. Presently Radisson came up again. Gering understood, having heard the footsteps.

"I will make the trial," he said. "Can you give me no other weapon?"

"I have only the one," responded Radisson, not unselfish enough to give it up. His chief idea, after all, was to put Gering under obligation to him.

"I will do my best," said Gering.

Then he turned to the governor, who did not care to risk his life in the way of escape.

Gering tried the key, but it would not turn easily and he took it out again. Rubbing away the rust, he used tallow from the candle, and tried the lock again; still it would not turn. He looked to the fastenings, but they were solid, and he feared noise; he made one more attempt with the lock, and suddenly it turned. He tried the handle, and the door opened. Then he bade goodbye to the governor and stepped out, almost upon the guard, who was sound asleep. Looking round he saw Iberville's cloak, which its owner had thrown off in his sleep He stealthily picked it up, and then put Iberville's cap on his head. Of nearly the same height, with these disguises he might be able to pass for his captor.

He threw the cloak over his shoulders, stole silently to the hatchway, and cautiously climbed up. Thrusting out his head he looked about him, and he saw two or three figures bundled together at the mainmast--woodsmen who had celebrated victory too sincerely. He looked for the watch, but could not see him. Then he drew himself carefully up, and on his hands and knees passed to the starboard side and moved aft. Doing so he saw the watch start up from the capstan where he had been resting, and walk towards him. He did not quicken his pace. He trusted to his ruse--he would impersonate Iberville, possessed as he was of the hat and cloak. He moved to the bulwarks and leaned against them, looking into the water. The sentry was deceived; he knew the hat and cloak, and he was only too glad to have, as he thought, escaped the challenge of having slept at his post; so he began resolutely to pace the deck. Gering watched him closely, and moved deliberately to the stern. In doing so he suddenly came upon a body. He stopped and turned round, leaning against the bulwarks as before. This time the watch came within twenty feet of him, saluted and retired.

Immediately Gering looked again at the body near him, and started back, for his feet were in a little pool. He understood: Radisson had escaped by killing his guard. It was not possible that the crime and the escape could go long undetected; the watch might at any moment come the full length of the ship. Gering flashed a glance at him again, his back was to him still,-- suddenly doffed the hat and cloak, vaulted lightly upon the bulwarks, caught the anchor-chain, slid down it into the water, and struck out softly along the side. Immediately Radisson was beside him.

"Can you dive?" the Frenchman whispered. "Can you swim under water?"

"A little."

"Then with me, quick!"

The Frenchman dived and Gering followed him. The water was bitter cold, but when a man is saving his life endurance multiplies.

The Fates were with them: no alarm came from the ship, and they reached the bank in safety. Here they were upon a now hostile shore without food, fire, shelter, and weapons; their situation was desperate even yet. Radisson's ingenuity was not quite enough, so Gering solved the problem: there were the Frenchmen's canoes; they must be somewhere on the shore. Because Radisson was a Frenchman, he might be able to impose upon the watch guarding the canoes. If not, they still had weapons of a kind- Radisson a knife, and Gering the bar of iron. They moved swiftly along the shore, fearing an alarm meanwhile. If they could but get weapons and a canoe they would make their way either to Fort Albany, so warning it, or attempt the desperate journey to New York. Again fortune was with them. As it chanced, the watch, suffering from the cold night air, had gone into the bush to bring wood for firing. The two refugees stole near, and in the very first canoe found three muskets, and there were also bags filled with food. They hastily pushed out a canoe, got in, and were miles away before their escape was discovered.

Radisson was for going south at once to New York, but Gering would not hear of it, and at the mouth of a musket Radisson obeyed. They reached Fort Albany and warned it. Having thus done his duty towards the Hudson's Bay Company, and knowing that surrender must come, and that in this case his last state would be worse than his first, Gering proceeded with Radisson--hourly more hateful to him, yet to be endured for what had happened--southward upon the trail the Frenchmen had taken northward.

A couple of hours after Gering had thrown his hat and cloak into the blood of the coureur du bois, and slid down the anchor-chain, Iberville knew that his quarry was flown. The watch had thought that Iberville had gone below, and he had again relaxed, but presently a little maggot of wonder got into his brain. He then went aft. Dawn was just breaking; the grey moist light shone with a naked coldness on land and water; wild-fowl came fluttering, voiceless, past; night was still drenched in sleep. Suddenly he saw the dead body, and his boots dabbled in wet!

In all that concerned the honour of the arms of France and the conquest of the three forts, Hayes, Rupert, and Albany, Iberville might be content, but he chafed at, the escape of his enemies.

"I will not say it is better so, Pierre," urged De Casson; "but you have done enough for the king. Let your own cause come later."

"And it will come, abbe," he answered, with anger. "His account grows; we must settle all one day. And Radisson shall swing or I am no soldier --so!"

EPOCH THE THIRD

"AS WATER UNTO WINE"

THREE months afterwards George Gering was joyfully preparing to take two voyages. Perhaps, indeed, his keen taste for the one had much to do with his eagerness for the other--though most men find getting gold as cheerful as getting married. He had received a promise of marriage from Jessica, and he was also soon to start with William Phips for the Spaniards' country. His return to New York with the news of the capture of the Hudson's Bay posts brought consternation. There was no angrier man in all America than Colonel Richard Nicholls; there was perhaps no girl in all the world more agitated than Jessica, then a guest at Government House. Her father was there also, cheerfully awaiting her marriage with Gering, whom, since he had lost most traces of Puritanism, he liked. He had long suspected the girl's interest in Iberville; if he had known that two letters from him--unanswered--had been treasured, read, and re-read, he would have been anxious. That his daughter should marry a Frenchman--a filibustering seigneur, a Catholic, the enemy of the British colonies, whose fellow-countrymen incited the Indians to harass and to massacre--was not to be borne.

Besides, the Honourable Hogarth Leveret, whose fame in the colony was now often in peril because of his Cavalier propensities, and whose losses had aged him, could not bear that he should sink and carry his daughter with him. Jessica was the apple of his eye; for her he would have borne all, sorts of trials; but he could not bear to see her called on to bear them. Like most people out of the heyday of their own youth, he imagined the way a maid's fancy ought to go.

If he had known how much his daughter's promise to marry Gering would cost her, he would not have had it. But indeed she did not herself guess it. She had, with the dreamy pleasure of a young girl, dwelt upon an event which might well hold her delighted memory: distance, difference of race, language, and life, all surrounded Iberville with an engaging fascination. Besides, what woman could forget a man who gave her escape from a fate such as Bucklaw had prepared for her? But she saw the hopelessness of the thing, everything was steadily acting in Gering's favour, and her father's trouble decided her at last.

When Gering arrived at New York and told his story--to his credit with no dispraise of Iberville, rather as a soldier--she felt a pang greater than she ever had known. Like a good British maid, she was angry at the defeat of the British, she was indignant at her lover's failure and proud of his brave escape, and she would have herself believe that she was angry at Iberville. But it was no use; she was ill-content while her father and others called him buccaneer and filibuster, and she joyed that old William Drayton, who had ever spoken well of the young Frenchman, laughed at their insults, saying that he was as brave, comely, and fine-tempered a lad as he had ever met, and that the capture of the forts was genius: "Genius and pith, upon my soul!" he said stoutly; "and if he comes this way he shall have a right hearty welcome, though he come to fight."

In the first excitement of Gering's return, sorry for his sufferings and for his injured ambition, she had suddenly put her hands in his and had given her word to marry him.

She was young, and a young girl does not always know which it is that moves her: the melancholy of the impossible, from which she sinks in a kind of peaceful despair upon the possible, or the flush of a deep desire; she acts in an atmosphere of the emotions, and cannot therefore be sure of herself. But when it was done there came reaction to Jessica. In the solitude of her own room--the room above the hallway, from which she had gone to be captured by Bucklaw--she had misgivings. If she had been asked whether she loved Iberville, she might have answered no. But he was a possible lover; and every woman weighs the possible lover against the accepted one--often, at first, to fluttering apprehensions. In this brief reaction many a woman's heart has been caught away.

A few days after Gering's arrival he was obliged to push on to Boston, there to meet Phips. He hoped that Mr. Leveret and Jessica would accompany him, but Governor Nicholls would not hear of it just yet. Truth is, wherever the girl went she was light and cheerfulness, although her ways were quiet and her sprightliness was mostly in her looks. She was impulsive, but impulse was ruled by a reserve at once delicate and unembarrassed. She was as much beloved in the town of New York as in Boston.

Two days after Gering left she was wandering in the garden, when the governor joined her.

"Well, well, my pretty councillor," he said--"an hour to cheer an old man's leisure?"

"As many as you please," she answered daintily, putting her hand within his arm. "I am so very cheerful I need to shower the surplus." There was a smile at her lips, but her eyes were misty. Large, brilliant, gentle, they had now also a bewildered look, which even the rough old soldier saw. He did not understand, but he drew the hand further within his arm and held it, there, and for the instant he knew not what to say. The girl did not speak; she only kept looking at him with a kind of inward smiling. Presently, as if he had suddenly lighted upon a piece of news for the difficulty, he said: "Radisson has come."

"Radisson!" she cried.

"Yes. You know 'twas he that helped George to escape?"

"Indeed, no!" she answered. "Mr. Gering did not tell me." She was perplexed, annoyed, yet she knew not why.

Gering had not brought Radisson into New York had indeed forbidden him to come there, or to Boston, until word was given him; for while he felt bound to let the scoundrel go with him to the Spaniards' country, it was not to be forgotten that the fellow had been with Bucklaw. But Radisson had no scruples when Gering was gone, though the proscription had never been withdrawn.

"We will have to give him freedom, councillor, eh? even though we proclaimed him, you remember." He laughed, and added: "You would demand that, yea or nay.

"Why should I?" she asked.

"Now, give me wisdom all ye saints! Why--why?

"Faith, he helped your lover from the clutches of the French coxcomb."

"Indeed," she answered, "such a villain helps but for absurd benefits. Mr. Gering might have stayed with Monsieur Iberville in honour and safety at least. And why a coxcomb? You thought different once; and you cannot doubt his bravery. Enemy of our country though he be, I am surely bound to speak him well--he saved my life."

Anxious to please her, he answered: "Wise as ever, councillor. What an old bear am I: When I called him coxcomb, 'twas as an Englishman hating a Frenchman, who gave our tongues to gall--a handful of posts gone, a ship passed to the spoiler, the governor of the company a prisoner, and our young commander's reputation at some trial! My temper was pardonable, eh, mistress?"

The girl smiled, and added: "There was good reason why Mr. Gering brought not Radisson here, and I should beware that man. A traitor is ever a traitor. He is French, too, and as a good Englishman you should hate all Frenchmen, should you not?"

"Merciless witch! Where got you that wit? If I must, I kneel;" and he groaned in mock despair. "And if Monsieur Iberville should come knocking at our door you would have me welcome him lovingly?"

"Surely; there is peace, is there not? Has not the king, because of his love for Louis commanded all goodwill between us and Canada?"

The governor laughed bitterly. "Much pity that he has! how can we live at peace with buccaneers?" Their talk was interrupted here; but a few days later, in the same garden, Morris came to them. "A ship enters harbour," he said, "and its commander sends this letter."

An instant after the governor turned a troubled face on the girl and said: "Your counsel of the other day is put to rapid test, Jessica. This comes from monsieur, who would pay his respects to me."

He handed the note to her. It said that Iberville had brought prisoners whom he was willing to exchange for French prisoners in the governor's hands.

Entering New York harbour with a single vessel showed in a strong light Iberville's bold, almost reckless, courage. The humour of it was not lost on Jessica, though she turned pale, and the paper fluttered in her fingers.

"What will you do?" she said.

"I will treat him as well as he will let me, sweetheart." Two hours afterwards, Iberville came up the street with Sainte-Helene, De Casson, and Perrot,--De Troyes had gone to Quebec,--courteously accompanied by Morris and an officer of the New York Militia. There was no enmity shown the Frenchmen, for many remembered what had once made Iberville popular in New York. Indeed, Iberville, whose memory was of the best, now and again accosted some English or Dutch resident, whose face he recalled.

The governor was not at first cordial; but Iberville's cheerful soldierliness, his courtier spirit, and his treatment of the English prisoners, soon placed him on a footing near as friendly as that of years before. The governor praised his growing reputation, and at last asked him to dine, saying that Mistress Leveret would no doubt be glad to meet her rescuer again.

"Still, I doubt not," said the governor, "there will be embarrassment, for the lady can scarce forget that you had her lover prisoner. But these things are to be endured. Besides, you and Mr. Gering seem as easily enemies as other men are friends."

Iberville was amazed. So, Jessica and Gering were affianced. And the buckle she had sent him he wore now in the folds of his lace! How could he know what comes from a woman's wavering sympathies, what from her inborn coquetry, and what from love itself? He was merely a man with much to learn.

He accepted dinner and said: "As for Monsieur Gering, your excellency, we are as easily enemies as he and Radisson are comrades-in-arms."

"Which is harshly put, monsieur. When a man is breaking prison he chooses any tool. You put a slight upon an honest gentleman."

"I fear that neither Mr. Gering nor myself is too generous with each other, your excellency," answered Iberville lightly.

This frankness was pleasing, and soon the governor took Iberville into the drawing-room, where Jessica was. She was standing by the great fireplace, and she did not move at first, but looked at Iberville in some thing of her old simple way. Then she offered him her hand with a quiet smile.

"I fear you are not glad to see me," he said, with a smile. "You cannot have had good reports of me--no?"

"Yes, I am glad," she answered gently. "You know, monsieur, mine is a constant debt. You do not come to me, I take it, as the conqueror of Englishmen."

"I come to you," he answered, "as Pierre le Moyne of Iberville, who had once the honour to do you slight service. I have never tried to forget that, because by it I hoped I might be remembered--an accident of price to me."

She bowed and at first did not speak; then Morris came to say that some one awaited the governor, and the two were left alone.

"I have not forgotten," she began softly, breaking a silence.

"You will think me bold, but I believe you will never forget," was his meaning reply.

"Yes, you are bold," she replied, with the demure smile which had charmed him long ago. Suddenly she looked up at him anxiously, and, "Why did you go to Hudson's Bay?" she asked.

"I would have gone ten times as far for the same cause," he answered, and he looked boldly, earnestly, into her eyes.

She turned her head away. "You have all your old recklessness," she answered. Then her eyes softened, and, "All your old courage," she added.

"I have all my old motive."

"What is-your motive?"

Does a woman ever know how much such speeches cost? Did Jessica quite know when she asked the question, what her own motive was; how much it had of delicate malice--unless there was behind it a simple sincerity? She was inviting sorrow. A man like Iberville was not to be counted lightly; for every word he sowed, he would reap a harvest of some kind.

He came close to her, and looked as though he would read her through and through. "Can you ask that question?" he said most seriously. "If you ask it because from your soul you wish to know, good! But if you ask it as a woman who would read a man's heart, and then--"

"Oh, hush!--hush!" she whispered. Her face became pale, and her eyes had a painful brightness. "You must not answer. I had no right to ask. Oh, monsieur!" she added, "I would have you always for my friend if I could, though you are the enemy of my country and of the man--I am to marry."

"I am for my king," he replied; "and I am enemy of him who stands between you and me. For see: from the hour that I met you I knew that some day, even as now, I should tell you that--I love you--indeed, Jessica, with all my heart."

"Oh, have pity!" she pleaded. "I cannot listen--I cannot."

"You shall listen, for you have remembered me and have understood. Voila!" he added, hastily catching her silver buckle from his bosom. "This that you sent me, look where I have kept it--on my heart!"

She drew back from him, her face in her hands. Then suddenly she put them out as though to prevent him coming near her, and said:

"Oh, no--no! You will spare me; I am an affianced wife." An appealing smile shone through her tears. "Oh, will you not go?" she begged. "Or, will you not stay and forget what you have said? We are little more than strangers; I scarcely know you; I--"

"We are no strangers," he broke in. "How can that be, when for years I have thought of you--you of me? But I am content to wait, for my love shall win you yet. You--"

She came to him and put her hands upon his arm. "You remember," she said, with a touch of her old gaiety, and with an inimitable grace, "what good friends we were that first day we met? Let us be the same now--for this time at least. Will you not grant me this for to-day?"

"And to-morrow?" he asked, inwardly determining to stay in the port of New York and to carry her off as his wife; but, unlike Bucklaw, with her consent.

At that moment the governor returned, and Iberville's question was never answered. Nor did he dine at Government House, for word came secretly that English ships were coming from Boston to capture him. He had, therefore, no other resource but to sail out and push on for Quebec. He would not peril the lives of his men merely to follow his will with Jessica.

What might have occurred had he stayed is not easy to say--fortunes turn on strange trifles. The girl, under the influence of his masterful spirit and the rare charm of his manner, might have--as many another has --broken her troth. As it was, she wrote Iberville a letter and sent it by a courier, who never delivered it. By the same fatality, of the letters which he wrote her only one was received. This told her that when he returned from a certain cruise he would visit her again, for he was such an enemy to her country that he was keen to win what did it most honour. Gering had pressed for a marriage before he sailed for the Spaniards' country, but she had said no, and when he urged it she had shown a sudden coldness. Therefore, bidding her good-bye, he had sailed away with Phips, accompanied, much against his will, by Radisson. Bucklaw was not with them. He had set sail from England in a trading schooner, and was to join Phips at Port de la Planta. Gering did not know that Bucklaw had share in the expedition, nor did Bucklaw guess the like of Gering.

Within two weeks of the time that Phips in his Bridgwater Merchant, manned by a full crew, twenty fighting men, and twelve guns, with Gering in command of the Swallow, a smaller ship, got away to the south, Iberville also sailed in the same direction. He had found awaiting him, on his return to Quebec, a priest bearing messages and a chart from another priest who had died in the Spaniards' country.

IN WHICH THE HUNTERS ARE OUT

IBERVILLE had a good ship. The Maid of Provence carried a handful of guns and a small but carefully chosen crew, together with Sainte-Helene, Perrot, and the lad Maurice Joval, who had conceived for Iberville friendship nigh to adoration. Those were days when the young were encouraged to adventure, and Iberville had no compunction in giving the boy this further taste of daring.

Iberville, thorough sailor as he was, had chosen for his captain one who had sailed the Spanish Main. He had commanded on merchant-ships which had been suddenly turned into men-of-war, and was suited to the present enterprise: taciturn, harsh of voice, singularly impatient, but a perfect seaman and as brave as could be. He had come to Quebec late the previous autumn with the remnants of a ship which, rotten when she left the port of Havre, had sprung a leak in mid-ocean, had met a storm, lost her mainmast, and by the time she reached the St. Lawrence had scarce a stick standing. She was still at Quebec, tied up in the bay of St. Charles, from which she would probably go out no more. Her captain--Jean Berigord --had chafed on the bit in the little Hotel Colbert, making himself more feared than liked, till one day he was taken to Iberville by Perrot.

A bargain was soon struck. The nature of the expedition was not known in Quebec, for the sailors were not engaged till the eve of starting, and Perrot's men were ready at his bidding without why or wherefore. Indeed, when the Maid of Provence left the island of Orleans, her nose seawards, one fine July morning, the only persons in Quebec that knew her destina-tion were the priest who had brought Iberville the chart of the river, with its accurate location of the sunken galleon, Iberville's brothers, and Count Frontenac himself--returned again as governor.

"See, Monsieur Iberville," said the governor, as, with a fine show of compliment, in full martial dress, with his officers in gold lace, perukes, powder, swords, and ribbons, he bade Iberville good-bye--"See, my dear captain, that you find the treasure, or make these greedy English pay dear for it. They have a long start, but that is nothing, with a ship under you that can show its heels to any craft. I care not so much about the treasure, but I pray you humble those dull Puritans, who turn buccaneers in the name of the Lord."

Iberville made a gallant reply, and, with Sainte-Helene, received a hearty farewell from the old soldier, who, now over seventy years of age, was as full of spirit as when he distinguished himself at Arras fifty years before. In Iberville he saw his own youth renewed, and foretold the high part he would yet play in the fortunes of New France. Iberville had got to the door and was bowing himself out when, with a quick gesture, Frontenac stopped him, stepped quickly forward, and clasping his shoulders kissed him on each cheek, and said in a deep, kind voice: "I know, mon enfant, what lies behind this. A man pays the price one time or another: he draws his sword for his mistress and his king; both forget, but one's country remains-- remains."

Iberville said nothing, but with an admiring glance into the aged, iron face, stooped and kissed Frontenac's hand and withdrew silently. Frontenac, proud, impatient, tyrannical, was the one man in New France who had a powerful idea of the future of the country, and who loved her and his king by the law of a loyal nature. Like Wolsey, he had found his king ungrateful, and had stood almost alone in Canada among his enemies, as at Versailles among his traducers--imperious, unyielding, and yet forgiving. Married, too, at an early age, his young wife, caring little for the duties of maternity and more eager to serve her own ambitions than his, left him that she might share the fortunes of Mademoiselle de Montpensier.

Iberville had mastered the chart before he sailed, and when they were well on their way he disclosed to the captain the object of their voyage. Berigord listened to all he had to say, and at first did no more than blow tobacco smoke hard before him. "Let me see the chart," he said at last, and, scrutinising it carefully, added: "Yes, yes, 'tis right enough. I've been in the port and up the river. But neither we nor the Eng lish'll get a handful of gold or silver thereabouts. 'Tis throwing good money after none at all."

"The money is mine, my captain," said Iberville good-humouredly. "There will be sport, and I ask but that you give me every chance you can."

"Look then, monsieur," replied the smileless man, "I'll run your ship for all she holds from here to hell, if you twist your finger. She's as good a craft as ever I spoke, and I'll swear her for any weather. The fighting and the gold as you and the devil agree!"

Iberville wished nothing better--a captain concerned only with his own duties. Berigord gathered the crew and the divers on deck, and in half a dozen words told them the object of the expedition, and was followed by Iberville. Some of the men had been with him to Hudson's Bay, and they wished nothing better than fighting the English, and all were keen with the lust of gold even though it were for another. As it was, Iberville promised them all a share of what was got.

On the twentieth day after leaving Quebec they sighted islands, and simultaneously they saw five ships bearing away towards them. Iberville was apprehensive that a fleet of the kind could only be hostile, for merchant-ships would hardly sail together so, and it was not possible that they were French. There remained the probability that they were Spanish or English ships. He had no intention of running away, but at the same time he had no wish to fight before he reached Port de la Planta and had had his hour with Gering and Phips and the lost treasure. Besides, five ships was a large undertaking, which only a madman would willingly engage. However, he kept steadily on his course. But there was one chance of avoiding a battle without running away--the glass had been falling all night and morning. Berigord, when questioned, grimly replied that there was to be trouble, but whether with the fleet or the elements was not clear, and Iberville did not ask.

He got his reply effectively and duly however. A wind suddenly sprang up from the north-west, followed by a breaking cross sea. It as suddenly swelled to a hurricane, so that if Berigord had not been fortunate as to his crew, and had not been so fine a sailor, the Maid of Provence might have fared badly, for he kept all sail on as long as he dare, and took it in none too soon. But so thoroughly did he know the craft and trust his men that she did what he wanted; and though she was tossed and hammered by the sea till it seemed that she must, with every next wave, go down, she rode into safety at last, five hundred miles out of their course.

The storm had saved them from the hostile fleet, which had fared ill. They were first scattered, then two of them went down, another was so disabled that she had to be turned back to the port they had left, and the remaining two were separated, so that their only course was to return to port also.

As the storm came up they had got within fighting distance of the Maid of Provence, and had opened ineffectual fire, which she-- occupied with the impact of the storm--did not return. Escaped the dangers of the storm, she sheered into her course again, and ran away to the south-west, until Hispaniola came in sight.

IN THE MATTER OF BUCKLAW

THE Bridgwater Merchant and the Swallow made the voyage down with no set-backs, having fair weather and a sweet wind on their quarter all the way, to the wild corner of an island, where a great mountain stands sentinel and a bay washes upon a curving shore and up the. River de la Planta. There were no vessels in the harbour and there was only a small settlement on the shore, and as they came to anchor well away from the gridiron of reefs known as the Boilers, the prospect was handsome: the long wash of the waves, the curling, white of the breakers, and the rainbow-coloured water. The shore was luxuriant, and the sun shone intemperately on the sea and the land, covering all with a fine beautiful haze, like the most exquisite powder sifted through the air. All on board the Bridgwater Merchant and the Swallow were in hearty spirits. There had been some sickness, but the general health of the expedition was excellent.

It was not till the day they started from Boston that Phips told Gering he expected to meet some one at the port who had gone to prepare the way, to warn them by fires in case of danger, and to allay any opposition among the natives--if there were any. But he had not told him who the herald was.

Truth is, Phips was anxious that Gering should have no chance of objecting to the scoundrel who had, years before, tried to kidnap his now affianced wife--who had escaped a deserved death on the gallows. It was a rude age, and men of Phips's quality, with no particular niceness as to women, or horror as to mutiny when it was twenty years old, compromised with their conscience for expediency and gain. Moreover, in his humorous way, Bucklaw, during his connection with Phips in England, had made himself agreeable and resourceful. Phips himself had sprung from the lower orders,--the son of a small farmer,--and even in future days when he rose to a high position in the colonies, gaining knighthood and other honours, he had the manners and speech of "a man of the people." Bucklaw understood men: he knew that his only game was that of bluntness. This was why he boarded Phips in Cheapside without subterfuge or disguise.

Nor had Phips told Bucklaw of Gering's coming; so that when the Bridgwater Merchant and the Swallow entered Port de la Planta, Bucklaw himself, as he bore out in a small sail-boat, did not guess that he was likely to meet a desperate enemy. He had waited patiently, and had reckoned almost to a day when Phips would arrive. He was alongside before Phips had called anchor. His cheerful countenance came up between the frowning guns, his hook-hand ran over the rail, and in a moment he was on deck facing-- Radisson.

He was unprepared for the meeting, but he had taken too many chances in his lifetime to show astonishment. He and Radisson had fought and parted; they had been in ugly business together, and they were likely to be, now that they had met, in ugly business again.

Bucklaw's tiger ran up to stroke his chin with the old grotesque gesture. "Ha!" he said saucily, "cats and devils have nine lives."

There was the same sparkle in the eye as of old, the same buoyant voice. For himself, he had no particular quarrel with Radisson; the more so because he saw a hang-dog sulkiness in Radisson's eye. It was ever his cue when others were angered to be cool. The worst of his crimes had been performed with an air of humorous cynicism. He could have great admiration for an enemy such as Iberville; and he was not a man to fight needlessly. He had a firm belief that he had been intended for a high position--a great admiral, or general, or a notable buccaneer.

Before Radisson had a chance to reply came Phips, who could not help but show satisfaction at Bucklaw's presence; and in a moment they were on their way together to the cabin, followed by the eyes of the enraged Radisson. Phips disliked Radisson; the sinister Frenchman, with his evil history, was impossible to the open, bluff captain. He had been placed upon Phips's vessel because he knew the entrance to the harbour; but try as he would for a kind of comradeship, he failed: he had an ugly vanity and a bad heart. There was only one decent thing which still clung to him in rags and tatters--the fact that he was a Frenchman. He had made himself hated on the ship--having none of the cunning tact of Bucklaw. As Phips and Bucklaw went below, a sudden devilry entered into him. He was ripe for quarrel, eager for battle. His two black eyes were like burning beads, his jaws twitched. If Bucklaw had but met him without this rough, bloodless irony, he might have thrown himself with ardour into the work of the expedition; but he stood alone, and hatred and war rioted in him.

Below in the cabin Phips and Bucklaw were deep in the chart of the harbour and the river. The plan of action was decided upon. A canoe was to be built out of a cotton-tree large enough to carry eight or ten oars. This and the tender, with men and divers, were to go in search of the wreck under the command of Bucklaw and the captain of the Swallow, whose name Phips did not mention. Phips himself was to remain on the Bridgwater Merchant, the Swallow lying near with a goodly number of men to meet any possible attack from the sea. When all was planned, Phips told Bucklaw who was the commander of the Swallow. For a moment the fellow's coolness was shaken; the sparkle died out of his eye and he shot up a furtive look at Phips, but he caught a grim smile on the face of the sturdy sailor. He knew at once there was no treachery meant, and he guessed that Phips expected no crisis. It was ever his way to act with promptness, being never so resourceful as when his position was most critical: he was in the power of Gering and Phips, and he knew it, but he knew also that his game must be a bold one.

"By-gones are by-gones, captain," he said; "and what's done can't be helped, and as it was no harm came anyhow."

"By-gones are by-gones," replied the other, "and let's hope that Mr. Gering will say so too."

"Haven't you told him, sir?"

"Never a word--but I'll send for him now, and bygones let it be."

Bucklaw nodded, and drummed the table with his tiger. He guessed why Phips had not told Gering, and he foresaw trouble. He trusted, however, to the time that had passed since the kidnapping, and on Gering's hunger for treasure. Phips had compromised, and why not he? But if Gering was bent on trouble, why, there was the last resource of the peace-lover. He tapped the rapier at his side. He ever held that he was peaceful, and it is recorded that at the death of an agitated victim, he begged him to "sit still and not fidget."

He laid no plans as to what he should do when Gering came. Like the true gamester, he waited to see how he should be placed; then he could draw upon his resources. He was puzzled about Radisson, but Radisson could wait; he was so much the superior of the coarser villain that he gave him little thought. As he waited he thought more about the treasure at hand than of either--or all--his enemies.

He did not stir, but kept drumming till he knew that Gering was aboard, and heard his footsteps, with the captain's, coming. He showed no excitement, though he knew a crisis was at hand. A cool, healthy sweat stood out on his forehead, cheeks and lips, and his blue eyes sparkled clearly and coldly. He rose as the two men appeared.

Phips had not even told his lieutenant. But Gering knew Bucklaw at the first glance, and his eyes flashed and a hand went to his sword.

"Captain Phips," he said angrily, "you know who this man is?"

"He is the guide to our treasure-house, Mr. Gering."

"His name is Bucklaw--a mutineer condemned to death, the villain who tried to kidnap Mistress Leveret."

It was Bucklaw that replied. "Right--right you are, Mr. Gering. I'm Bucklaw, mutineer, or what else you please. But that's ancient--ancient. I'm sinner no more. You and Monsieur Iberville saved the maid I meant no harm to her; 'twas but for ransom. I am atoning now--to make your fortune, give you glory. Shall by-gones be by-gones, Mr. Gering? What say you?"

Bucklaw stood still at the head of the table. But he was very watchful. What the end might have been it is hard to tell, but a thing occurred which took the affair out of Gering's hands.

A shadow darkened the companion-way, and Radisson came quickly down. His face was sinister, and his jaws worked like an animal's. Coming to the table he stood between Gering and Bucklaw, and looked from one to the other. Bucklaw was cool, Gering very quiet, and he misinterpreted.

"You are great friends, eh, all together?" he said viciously. "All together you will get the gold. It is no matter what one English do, the other absolve for gold. A buccaneer, a stealer of women--no, it is no matter! All English--all together! But I am French--I am the dirt-- I am for the scuppers. Bah! I will have the same as Bucklaw--you see?"

"You will have the irons, fellow!" Phips roared.

A knife flashed in the air, and Bucklaw's pistol was out at the same instant. The knife caught Bucklaw in the throat and he staggered against the table like a stuck pig, the bullet hit Radisson in the chest and he fell back against the wall, his pistol dropping from his hand. Bucklaw, bleeding heavily, lurched forwards, pulled himself together, and, stooping, emptied his pistol into the moaning Radisson. Then he sank on his knees, snatched the other's pistol, and fired again into Radisson's belly; after which with a last effort he plunged his own dagger into the throat of the dying man, and, with his fingers still on the handle, fell with a gurgling laugh across the Frenchman's body.

Radisson recovered for an instant. He gave a hollow cry, drew the knife from his own throat and, with a wild, shambling motion, struck at the motionless Bucklaw, pinning an arm to the ground. Then he muttered an oath and fell back dead.

The tournament of blood was over. So swift had it been there was no chance to interfere. Besides, Gering was not inclined to save the life of either; while Phips, who now knew the chart, as he thought, as well as Bucklaw, was not concerned, though he liked the mutineer.

For a moment they both looked at the shambles without speaking. Sailors for whom Phips had whistled crowded the cabin.

"A damned bad start, Mr. Gering," Phips said, as he moved towards the bodies.

"For them, yes; but they might have given us a bad ending."

"For the Frenchman, he's got less than was brewing for him, but Bucklaw was a humorous dog."

As he said this he stooped to Bucklaw and turned him over, calling to the sailors to clean the red trough and bring the dead men on deck, but presently he cried: "By the devil's tail, the fellow lives! Here, a hand quick, you lubbers, and fetch the surgeon."

Bucklaw was not dead. He had got two ugly wounds and was bleeding heavily, but his heart still beat. Radisson's body was carried on deck, and within half an hour was dropped into the deep. The surgeon, however, would not permit Bucklaw to be removed until he had been cared for, and so Phips and Gering went on deck and made preparations for the treasure-hunt. A canoe was hollowed out by a dozen men in a few hours, the tender was got ready, the men and divers told off, and Gering took command of the searching-party, while Phips remained on the ship.

They soon had everything ready for a start in the morning. Word was brought that Bucklaw still lived, but was in a high fever, and that the chances were all against him; and Phips sent cordials and wines from his own stores, and asked that news be brought to him of any change.

Early in the morning Gering, after having received instructions from Phips, so far as he knew (for Bucklaw had not told all that was necessary), departed for the river. The canoe and tender went up the stream a distance, and began to work down from the farthest point indicated in the chart. Gering continued in the river nearly all day, and at night camped on the shore. The second day brought no better luck, nor yet the third the divers had seen no vestige of a wreck, nor any sign of treasure--nothing except four skeletons in a heap, tied together with a chain, where the water was deepest. These were the dead priests, for whom Bucklaw could account. The water was calm, the tide rising and falling gently, and when they arrived among what was called the Shallows, they could see plainly to the bottom. They passed over the Boilers, a reef of shoals, and here they searched diligently, but to no purpose; the divers went down frequently, but could find nothing. The handful of natives in the port came out and looked on apathetically; one or two Spaniards also came, but they shrugged their shoulders and pitied the foolish adventurers. Gering had the power of inspiring his men, and Phips was a martinet and was therefore obeyed; but the lifeless days and unrewarded labour worked on the men, and at last the divers shirked their task.

Meanwhile, Bucklaw was fighting hard for life.

As time passed, the flush of expectancy waned; the heat was great, the waiting seemed endless. Adventure was needed for the spirits of the men, and of this now there was nothing. Morning after morning the sun rose in a moist, heavy atmosphere; day after day went in a quest which became dreary, and night after night settled upon discontent. Then came threats. But this was chiefly upon the Bridgwater Merchant. Phips had picked up his sailors in English ports, and nearly all of them were brutal adventurers. They were men used to desperate enterprises, and they had flocked to him because they smelled excitement and booty. Of ordinary merchant seamen there were only a few. When the Duke of Albemarle had come aboard at Plymouth before they set sail, he had shrugged his shoulders at the motley crew. To his hint Phips had only replied with a laugh: these harum-scarum scamps were more to his mind than ordinary seamen. At heart he himself was half-barbarian. It is possible he felt there might some time be a tug-of-war on board, but he did not borrow trouble. Bucklaw had endorsed every man that he had chosen; indeed, Phips knew that many of them were old friends of Bucklaw. Again, of this he had no fear; Bucklaw was a man of desperate deeds, but he knew that in himself the pirate had a master. Besides, he would pick up in Boston a dozen men upon whom he could depend; and cowardice had no place in him. Again, the Swallow, commanded by Gering, was fitted out with New England seamen; and on these dependence could be put.

Therefore, when there came rumblings of mutiny on the Bridgwater Merchant, there was faithful, if gloomy, obedience, on the Swallow. Had there been plenty of work to do, had they been at sea instead of at anchor, the nervousness would have been little; but idleness begot irritation, and irritation mutiny. Or had Bucklaw been on deck, instead of in the surgeon's cabin playing a hard game with death, matters might not have gone so far as they did; for he would have had immediate personal influence repressive of revolt. As it was, Phips had to work the thing out according to his own lights. One afternoon, when Gering was away with the canoes on the long search, the crisis came. It was a day when life seemed to stand still; a creamy haze ingrained with delicate blue had settled on land and sea; the long white rollers slowly travelled over the Boilers, and the sea rocked like a great cradle. Indefiniteness of thought, of time, of event, seemed over all; on board the two ships life swung idly as a hammock; but only so in appearance.

Phips was leaning against the deck-house, watching through his glass the search-canoes. Presently he turned and walked aft. As he did so the surgeon and the chief mate came running towards him. They had not time to explain, for came streaming upon deck a crowd of mutineers. Phips did not hesitate an instant; he had no fear--he was swelling with anger.

"Why now, you damned dogs," he blurted out, "what mean you by this? What's all this show of cutlasses?"

The ringleader stepped forwards. "We're sick of doing nothing," he answered. "We've come on a wild goose chase. There's no treasure here. We mean you no harm; we want not the ship out of your hands."

"Then," cried Phips, "in the name of all the devils, what want you?"

"Here's as we think: there's nothing to be got out of this hunt, but there's treasure on the high seas all the same. Here's our offer: keep command of your ship and run up the black flag!"

Phips's arm shot out and dropped the man to the ground.

"That's it, you filthy rogues!" he roared. "Me to turn pirate, eh? You'd set to weaving ropes for the necks of every one of us--blood of my soul!"

He seemed not to know that cutlasses were threatening him, not to be aware that the man at his feet, clutching his weapon, was mad with rage.

"Now look," he said, in a big loud voice, "I know that treasure is here, and I know we'll find it; if not now, when we get Bucklaw on his feet."

"Ay! Bucklaw! Bucklaw!" ran through the throng.

"Well, then, Bucklaw, as you say! Now here's what I'll do, scoundrels though you be. Let me hear no more of this foolery. Stick to me till the treasure's found--for God take my soul if I leave this bay till I have found it!--and you shall have good share of booty."

He had grasped the situation with such courage that the mutineers hesitated. He saw his advantage and followed it up, asking for three of their number to confer with him as to a bond upon his proposal. After a time the mutineers consented, the bond was agreed to, and the search went on.

IN THE TREASURE HOUSE

THE canoes and tender kept husking up and down among the Shallows, finding nothing. At last one morning they pushed out from the side of the Bridgwater Merchant, more limp than ever. The stroke of the oars was listless, but a Boston sailor of a merry sort came to a cheery song:

> "I knows a town, an' it's a fine town,
> And many a brig goes sailin' to its quay;
> I knows an inn, an' it's a fine inn,
> An' a lass that's fair to see.
> I knows a town, an' it's a fine town;
> I knows an inn, an' it's a fine inn
> But O my lass! an' O the gay gown,
> Which I have seen my pretty in!
>
> "I knows a port, an' it's a good port,
> An' many a brig is ridin' easy there;
> I knows a home, an' it's a good home,
> An' a lass that's sweet an' fair.
> I knows a port, an' it's a good port,
> I knows a home, an' it's a good home
> But O the pretty that is my sort,
> That's wearyin' till I come!
>
> "I knows a day, an' it's a fine day,
> The day a sailor man comes back to town.
> I knows a tide, an' it's a good tide,
> The tide that gets you quick to anchors down.
> I knows a day, an' it's a fine day,
> I knows a tide, an' its' a good tide
> And God help the lubber, I say,
> That's stole the sailor man's bride!"

The song had its way with them and they joined in and lay to their oars with almost too much goodwill. Gering, his arms upon the side of the canoe, was looking into the water idly. It was clear far down, and presently he saw what seemed a feather growing out of the side of a rock. It struck him as strange, and he gave word to back water. They were just outside the Boilers in deep water. Drawing back carefully, he saw the feather again, and ordered one of the divers to go down. They could see the man descend and gather the feather, then he plunged deeper still and they lost sight of him. But soon he came up rapidly, and was quickly inside the boat, to tell Gering that he had seen several great guns. At this the crew peered over the boat-side eagerly. Gering's heart beat hard. He knew what it was to rouse wild hope and then to see despair follow, but he kept an outward calm and told the diver to go down again. Time seemed to stretch to hours before they saw the man returning with something in his arm. He handed up his prize, and behold it was a pig of silver!

The treasure was found; and there went up a great cheer. All was activity, for, apart from the delight of discovery, Phips had promised a share to every man. The place was instantly buoyed, and they hastened back to the port with the grateful tidings to Phips. With his glass he saw them coming and by their hard rowing he guessed that they had news. When they came within hail they cheered, and when they saw the silver the air rang with shouts.

As Gering stepped on board with the silver Captain Phips ran forwards, clasped it in both hands, and cried: "We are all made, thanks be to God!"

Then all hands were ordered on board, and because the treasure lay in a safe anchorage they got the ships away towards it.

Bucklaw, in the surgeon's cabin, was called out of delirium by the noise. He was worn almost to a skeleton, his eyes were big and staring, his face had the paleness of death. The return to consciousness was sudden-- perhaps nothing else could have called him back. He wriggled out of bed and, supporting himself against the wall, made his way to the door, and crawled away, mumbling to himself as he went.

A few minutes afterwards Phips and Gering were talking in the cabin. Phips was weighing the silver up and down in his hands.

"At least three hundred good guineas here!" he said. There was a shuffling behind them, and, as Phips turned, a figure lunged on him, clutched and hugged the silver. It was Bucklaw.

"Mine! mine!" he called in a hoarse voice, with great gluttonous eyes. "All mine!" he cried again. Then he gasped and came to the ground in a heap, with the silver hugged in his arms. All at once he caught at his throat; the bandage of his wound fell away and there was a rush of blood over the silver. With a wild laugh he plunged face forward on the metal --and the blood of the dead Bucklaw consecrated the first-fruits of the treasure.

As the vessel rode up the harbour the body was dropped into the deep.

"Worse men--worse men, sir, bide with the king," said Phips to Gering. "A merry villain, that Bucklaw." The ship came to anchor at the buoys, and no time was lost. Divers were sent down, and by great good luck found the room where the bullion was stored. The number of divers was increased, and the work of raising the bullion went on all that day. There is nothing like the lust for gold in the hearts of men. From stem to stern of the Bridgwater Merchant and the Swallow, this wild will had its way. Work went on until the last moment of sun. That night talk was long and sleep short, and work was on again at sunrise. In three days they took up thirty-two tons of bullion. In the afternoon of the third day the store-room was cleared, and then they searched the hold. Here they found, cunningly distributed among the ballast, a great many bags of pieces-of-eight. These, having lain in the water so long, were crusted with a strong substance, which they had to break with iron bars. It was reserved for Phips himself to make the grand discovery. He donned a diving-suit and went below to the sunken galleon. Silver and gold had been found, but he was sure there were other treasures. After much searching he found, in a secret place of the captain's cabin, a chest which, on being raised and broken open, was found stocked with pearls, diamonds, and other precious stones.

And now the work was complete, and on board the Bridgwater Merchant was treasure to the sum of three hundred thousand pounds, and more. Joyfully did Phips raise anchor. But first he sent to the handful of people in the port a liberal gift of money and wine and provisions from the ship's stores. With a favourable breeze he got away agreeably, and was clear of the harbour and cleaving northwards before sunset--the Swallow leading the treasure-ship like a pilot. All was joy and hilarity; but there remained one small danger yet: they had raised their treasure unmolested, but could they bring it to Boston and on to England? Phips would have asked that question very seriously indeed had he known that the Maid of Provence was bowling out of the nor'-east towards the port which he had just left.

The Maid of Provence had had a perilous travel. Escaping the English war-ships, she fell in with a pirate craft. She closed with it, plugged it with cannon-shot, and drew off, then took the wind on her beam and came drifting down on her, boarded her and, after a swift and desperate fight, killed every pirate-rogue save one--the captain--whom for reasons they made a prisoner. Then they sank the rover, and got away to Port de la Planta as fast as they were able. But by reason of the storm and the fighting, and drifting out of their course, they had lost ten days; and thus it was they reached the harbour a few hours after the Bridgwater Merchant and the Swallow had left.

They waited till morning and sailed cautiously in to face disappointment. They quickly learned the truth from the natives. There was but one thing to do and Iberville lost no time. A few hours to get fresh water and fruit and to make some repairs, for the pirate had not been idle in the fight--and then Berigord gave the nose of the good little craft to the sea, and drove her on with an honest wind, like a hound upon the scent. Iberville was vexed, but not unduly; he had the temper of a warrior who is both artist and gamester. As he said to Perrot: "Well, Nick, they've saved us the trouble of lifting the treasure; we'll see now who shall beach it."

He guessed that the English ships would sail to Boston for better arming ere they ventured to the English Channel. He knew the chances were against him, but it was his cue to keep heart in his followers. For days they sailed without seeing a single ship; then three showed upon the horizon and faded away. They kept on, passing Florida and Carolina, hoping to reach Boston before the treasure-ships, and to rob them at their own door. Their chances were fair, for the Maid of Provence had proved swift, good-tempered, and a sweet sailer in bad waters.

Iberville had reckoned well. One evening, after a sail northwards as fine as the voyage down was dirty, they came up gently within forty miles of Boston, and then, because there was nothing else to do, went idling up and down all night, keeping watch. The next morning there was a mist in the air, which might become fog. Iberville had dreaded this; but he was to have his chance, for even when Berigord's face lowered most the look- out from the shrouds called down that he sighted two ships. They were making for the coast. All sail was put on, they got away to meet the newcomers, and they were not long in finding these to be their quarry.

Phips did not think that any ship would venture against them so near Boston, and could not believe the Maid of Provence an enemy. He thought her an English ship eager to welcome them, but presently he saw the white ensign of France at the mizzen, and a round shot rattled through the rigging of the Bridgwater Merchant.

But he was two to one, and the game seemed with him. No time was wasted. Phips's ships came to and stood alongside, and the gunners got to work. The Bridgwater Merchant was high in the water, and her shot at first did little damage to the Maid of Provence, which, having the advantage of the wind, came nearer and nearer. The Swallow, with her twenty-odd guns, did better work, and carried away the foremast of the enemy, killing several men. But Iberville came on slowly, and, anxious to dispose of the Swallow first, gave her broadsides between wind and water, so that soon her decks were spotted with dying men, her bulwarks broken in, and her mainmast gone. The cannonade was heard in Boston, from which, a few hours later, two merchantmen set out for the scene of action, each carrying good guns.

But the wind suddenly sank, and as the Maid of Provence, eager to close with the Bridgwater Merchant, edged slowly down, a fog came between, and the firing ceased on both sides. Iberville let his ship drift on her path, intent on a hand-to-hand fight aboard the Bridgwater Merchant; the grappling-irons were ready, and as they drifted there was silence.

Every eye was strained. Suddenly a shape sprang out of the grey mist, and the Maid of Provence struck. There was a crash of timbers as the bows of the Swallow--it was she--were stove in, and then a wild cry. Instantly she began to sink. The grappling-irons remained motionless on the Maid of Provence. Iberville heard a commanding voice, a cheer, and saw a dozen figures jump from the shattered bow towards the bow of his own ship intent on fighting, but all fell short save one. It was a great leap, but the Englishman made it, catching the chains, and scrambling on deck. A cheer greeted him-the Frenchmen could not but admire so brave a feat. The Englishman took no notice, but instantly turned to see his own ship lurch forwards and, without a sound from her decks, sink gently down to her grave. He stood looking at the place where she had been, but there was only mist. He shook his head and a sob rattled in his throat; his brave, taciturn crew had gone down without a cry. He turned and faced his enemies. They had crowded forwards--Iberville, Sainte-Helene, Perrot, Maurice Joval, and the staring sailors. He choked down his emotion and faced them all like an animal at bay as Iberville stepped forwards. Without a word Gering pointed to the empty scabbard at his side.

"No, pardon me," said Iberville drily, "not as our prisoner, monsieur. You have us at advantage; you will remain our guest."

"I want no quarter," said Gering proudly and a little sullenly.

"There can be no question of quarter, monsieur. You are only one against us all. You cannot fight; you saved your life by boarding us. Hospitality is sacred; you may not be a prisoner of war, for there is no war between our countries."

"You came upon a private quarrel?" asked Gering.

"Truly; and for the treasure--fair bone of fight between us."

There was a pause, in which Gering stood half turned from them, listening. But the Bridgwater Merchant had drifted away in the mist. Presently he turned again to Iberville with a smile defiant and triumphant. Iberville understood, but showed nothing of what he felt, and he asked Sainte-Helene to show Gering to the cabin.

When the fog cleared away there was no sign of the Bridgwater Merchant and Iberville, sure that she had made the port of Boston, and knowing that there must be English vessels searching for him, bore away to Quebec with Gering on board.

He parted from his rival the day they arrived--Perrot was to escort him a distance on his way to Boston. Gering thanked him for his courtesy.

"Indeed, then," said Iberville, "this is a debt--if you choose to call it so--for which I would have no thanks--no. For it would please me better to render accounts all at once some day, and get return in different form, monsieur."

"Monsieur," said Gering, a little grandly, "you have come to me three times; next time I will come to you."

"I trust that you will keep your word," answered Iberville, smiling.

That day Iberville, protesting helplessly, was ordered away to France on a man-of-war, which had rocked in the harbour of Quebec for a month awaiting his return. Even Frontenac himself could not help him, for the order had come from the French minister.

THE GIFT OF A CAPTIVE

FORTUNE had not been kind to Iberville, but still he kept a stoical cheerfulness. With the pride of a man who feels that he has impressed a woman, and knowing the strength of his purpose, he believed that Jessica should yet be his. Meanwhile matters should not lie still. In those days men made love by proxy, and Iberville turned to De Casson and Perrot.

The night before he started for France they sat together in a little house flanking the Chateau St. Louis. Iberville had been speaking.

"I know the strength of your feelings, Iberville," said De Casson, "but is it wise, and is it right?" Iberville made an airy motion with his hand. "My dear abbe, there is but one thing worth living for, and that is to follow your convictions. See: I have known you since you took me from my mother's last farewell. I have believed in you, cared for you, trusted you; we have been good comrades. Come, now, tell me: what would you think if my mind drifted! No, no, no! to stand by one's own heart is the gift of an honest man--I am a sad rogue, abbe, as you know, but I swear I would sooner let slip the friendship of King Louis himself than the hand of a good comrade. Well, my sword is for my king. I must obey him, I must leave my comrades behind, but I shall not forget, and they must not forget." At this he got to his feet, came over, laid a hand on the abbe's shoulder, and his voice softened: "Abbe, the woman shall be mine."

"If God wills so, Iberville." "He will, He will."

"Well," said Perrot, with a little laugh; "I think God will be good to a Frenchman when an Englishman is his foe."

"But the girl is English--and a heretic," urged the abbe helplessly.

Perrot laughed again. "That will make Him sorry for her."

Meanwhile Iberville had turned to the table, and was now reading a letter. A pleased look came on his face, and he nodded in satisfaction. At last he folded it up with a smile and sealed it. "Well," he said, "the English is not good, for I have seen my Shakespeare little this time back, but it will do--it must do. In such things rhetoric is nothing. You will take it, Perrot?" he said, holding up the letter.

Perrot reached out for it.

"And there is something more." Iberville drew from his finger a costly ring. It had come from the hand of a Spanish noble, whose place he had taken in Spain years before. He had prevented his men from despoiling the castle, and had been bidden to take what he would, and had chosen only this.

"Tell her," he said, "that it was the gift of a captive to me, and that it is the gift of a captive to her. For, upon my soul, I am prisoner to none other in God's world."

Perrot weighed the ring up and down in his hand. "Bien," he said, "monsieur, it is a fine speech, but I do not understand. A prisoner, eh? I remember when you were a prisoner with me upon the Ottawa. Only a boy --only a boy, but, holy Mother, that was different! I will tell her how you never gave up; how you went on the hunt after Grey Diver, the Iroquois. Through the woods, silent--silent for days and days, Indians all round us. Death in the brush, death in the tree-top, death from the river-bank. I said to you, Give up; but you kept on. Then there were days when there was no sleep--no rest--we were like ghosts. Sometimes we come to a settler's cabin and see it all smoking; sometimes to a fort and find only a heap of bones--and other things! But you would not give up; you kept on. What for? That Indian chief killed your best friend. Well, that was for hate; you keep on and on and on for hate--and you had your way with Grey Diver; I heard your axe crash in his skull. All for hate! And what will you do for love?--I will ask her what will you do for love. Ah, you are a great man-- but yes! I will tell her so."

"Tell her what you please, Perrot."

Iberville hummed an air as at some goodly prospect. Yet when he turned to the others again there grew a quick mist in his eyes. It was not so much the thought of the woman as of the men. There came to him with sudden force how these two comrades had been ever ready to sacrifice themselves for him, and he ready to accept the sacrifice. He was not ashamed of the mist, but he wondered that the thing had come to him all at once. He grasped the hands of both, shook them heartily, then dashed his fingers across his eyes, and with the instinct of every imperfect man,--that touch of the aboriginal in all of us, who must have a sign for an emotion, he went to a cabinet and out came a bottle of wine.

An hour after, Perrot left him at the ship's side.

They were both cheerful. "Two years, Perrot; two years!" he said.

"Ah, mon grand capitaine!"

Iberville turned away, then came back again. "You will start at once?"

"At once; and the abbe shall write."

Upon the lofty bank of the St. Lawrence, at the Sault au Matelot, a tall figure clad in a cassock stood and watched the river below. On the high cliff of Point Levis lights were showing, and fires burning as far off as the island of Orleans. And in that sweet curve of shore, from the St. Charles to Beauport, thousands of stars seemed shining. Nearer still, from the heights, there was the same strange scintillation; the great promontory had a coronet of stars. In the lower town there was like illumination, and out upon the river trailed long processions of light. It was the feast of good Sainte Anne de Beaupre. All day long had there been masses and proces-sions on land. Hundreds of Jesuits, with thousands of the populace, had filed behind the cross and the host. And now there was a candle in every window. Indians, half-breeds, coureurs du bois, native Canadians, seigneurs, and noblesse, were joining in the function. But De Casson's eyes were not for these. He was watching the lights of a ship that slowly made its way down the river among the canoes, and his eyes never left it till it had passed beyond the island of Orleans and was lost in the night.

"Mon cher!" he said, "mon enfant! She is not for him; she should not be. As a priest it were my duty to see that he should not marry her. As a man" he sighed--"as a man I would give my life for him."

He lifted his hand and made the sign of the cross towards that spot on the horizon whither Iberville had gone.

"He will be a great man some day," he added to himself--"a great man. There will be empires here, and when histories are written Pierre's shall be a name beside Frontenac's and La Salle's."

All the human affection of the good abbe's life centred upon Iberville. Giant in stature, so ascetic and refined was his mind, his life, that he had the intuition of a woman and, what was more, little of the bigotry of his brethren. As he turned from the heights, made his way along the cliff and down Mountain Street, his thoughts were still upon the same subject. He suddenly paused.

"He will marry the sword," he said, "and not the woman."

How far he was right we may judge if we enter the house of Governor Nicholls at New York one month later.

MAIDEN NO MORE

IT was late mid-summer, and just such an evening as had seen the attempted capture of Jessica Leveret years before. She sat at a window, looking out upon the garden and the river. The room was at the top of the house. It had been to her a kind of play-room when she had visited Governor Nicholls years before. To every woman memory is a kind of religion; and to Jessica as much as to any, perhaps more than to most, for she had imagination. She half sat, half knelt, her elbow on her knee, her soft cheek resting upon her firm, delicate hand. Her beauty was as fresh and sweet as on the day we first saw her. More, something deep and rich had entered into it. Her eyes had got that fine steadfastness which only deep tenderness and pride can give a woman: she had lived. She was smiling now, yet she was not merry; her brightness was the sunshine of a nature touched with an Arcadian simplicity. Such an one could not be wholly unhappy. Being made for others more than for herself, she had something of the divine gift of self-forgetfulness.

As she sat there, her eyes ever watching the river as though for some one she expected, there came from the garden beneath the sound of singing. It was not loud, but deep and strong:

> "As the wave to the shore, as the dew to the leaf,
> As the breeze to the flower,
> As the scent of a rose to the heart of a child, 343
> As the rain to the dusty land--
> My heart goeth out unto Thee--unto Thee!
> The night is far spent and the day is at hand.
>
> "As the song of a bird to the call of a star,
> As the sun to the eye,
> As the anvil of man to the hammers of God,
> As the snow to the north
> Is my word unto Thy word--to Thy word!
> The night is far spent and the day is at hand."

It was Morris who was singing. With growth of years had come increase of piety, and it was his custom once a week to gather about him such of the servants as would for the reading of Scripture.

To Jessica the song had no religious significance. By the time it had passed through the atmosphere of memory and meditation, it carried a different meaning. Her forehead dropped forward in her fingers, and remained so until the song ended. Then she sighed, smiled wistfully, and shook her head.

"Poor fellow! poor--Iberville!" she said, almost beneath her breath.

The next morning she was to be married. George Gering had returned to her, for the second time defeated by Iberville. He had proved himself a brave man, and, what was much in her father's sight, he was to have his share of Phips's booty. And what was still more, Gering had prevailed upon Phips to allow Mr. Leveret's investment in the first expedition to receive a dividend from the second. Therefore she was ready to fulfil her promise. Yet had she misgivings? For, only a few days before, she had sent for the old pastor at Boston, who had known her since she was a child. She wished, she said, to be married by him and no other at Governor Nicholls's house, rather than at her own home at Boston, where there was none other of her name.

The old pastor had come that afternoon, and she had asked him to see her that evening. Not long after Morris had done with singing there came a tapping at her door. She answered and old Pastor Macklin entered, a white-haired man of kindly yet stern countenance, by nature a gentleman, by practice a bigot. He came forward and took both her hands as she rose. "My dear young lady!" he said, and smiled kindly at her. After a word of greeting she offered him a chair, and came again to the window.

Presently she looked up and said very simply: "I am going to be married. You have known me ever since I was born: do you think I will make a good wife?"

"With prayer and chastening of the spirit, my daughter," he said.

"But suppose that at the altar I remembered another man?"

"A sin, my child, for which should be due sorrow." The girl smiled sadly. She felt poignantly how little he could help her.

"And if the man were a Catholic and a Frenchman?" she said.

"A papist and a Frenchman!" he cried, lifting up his hands. "My daughter, you ever were too playful. You speak of things impossible. I pray you listen." Jessica raised her hand as if to stop him and to speak herself, but she let him go on. With the least encouragement she might have told him all. She had had her moment of weakness, but now it was past. There are times when every woman feels she must have a confidant, or her heart will burst--have counsel or she will die. Such a time had come to Jessica. But she now learned, as we all must learn, that we live our dark hour alone.

She listened as in a dream to the kindly bigot. When he had finished, she knelt and received his blessing. All the time she wore that strange, quiet smile. Soon afterwards he left her.

She went again to the window. "A papist and a Frenchman--unpardonable sin!" she said into the distance. "Jessica, what a sinner art thou!"

Presently there was a tap, the door opened, and George Gering entered. She turned to receive him, but there was no great lighting of the face. He came quickly to her, and ran his arm round her waist. A great kindness looked out of her eyes. Somehow she felt herself superior to him--her love was less and her nature deeper. He pressed her fingers to his lips. "Of what were you thinking, Jessica?" he asked.

"Of what a sinner I am," she answered, with a sad kind of humour.

"What a villain must I be, then!" he responded. "Well, yes," she said musingly; "I think you are something of a villain, George."

"Well, well, you shall cure me of all mine iniquities," he said. "There will be a lifetime for it. Come, let us to the garden."

"Wait," she said. "I told you that I was a sinner, George; I want to tell you how."

"Tell me nothing; let us both go and repent," he rejoined, laughing, and he hurried her away. She had lost her opportunity.

Next morning she was married. The day was glorious. The town was garlanded, and there was not an English merchant or a Dutch burgher but wore his holiday dress. The ceremony ended, a traveller came among the crowd. He asked a hurried question or two and then edged away. Soon he made a stand under the trees, and, viewing the scene, nodded his head and said: "The abbe was right."

It was Perrot. A few hours afterwards the crowd had gone and the governor's garden was empty. Perrot still kept his watch under the tree, though why he could hardly say--his errand was useless now. But he had the gift of waiting. At last he saw a figure issue from a door and go down into the garden. He remembered the secret gate. He made a detour, reached it, and entered. Jessica was walking up and down in the pines. In an hour or so she was to leave for England. Her husband had gone to the ship to do some needful things, and she had stolen out for a moment's quiet. When Perrot faced her, she gave a little cry and started back. But presently she recovered, smiled at him, and said kindly: "You come suddenly, monsieur."

"Yet have I travelled hard and long," he answered.

"Yes?"

"And I have a message for you."

"A message?" she said abstractedly, and turned a little pale.

"A message and a gift from Monsieur Iberville." He drew the letter and the ring from his pocket and held them out, repeating Iberville's message. There was a troubled look in her eyes and she was trembling a little now, but she spoke clearly.

"Monsieur," she said, "you will tell Monsieur Iberville that I may not; I am married."

"So, madame," he said. "But I still must give my message." When he had done so he said: "Will you take the letter?" He held it out.

There was a moment's doubt and then she took it, but she did not speak.

"Shall I carry no message, madame?"

She hesitated. Then, at last: "Say that I wish him good fortune--with all my heart."

"Good fortune--ah, madame!" he answered, in a meaning tone.

"Say that I pray God may bless him, and make him a friend of my country," she added in a low, almost broken voice, and she held out her hand to him.

The gallant woodsman pressed it to his lips. "I am sorry, madame," he replied, with an admiring look.

She shook her head sadly. "Adieu, monsieur!" she said steadily and very kindly.

A moment after he was gone. She looked at the missive steadfastly for a moment, then thrust it into the folds of her dress and, very pale, walked quietly to the house, where, inside her own room, she lighted a candle. She turned the letter over in her hand once or twice, and her fingers hung at the seal. But all at once she raised it to her lips, and then with a grave, firm look, held it in the flame and saw it pass in smoke. It was the last effort for victory.

EPOCH THE FOURTH

WHICH TELLS OF A BROTHER'S BLOOD CRYING FROM THE GROUND

TWO men stood leaning against a great gun aloft on the heights of Quebec.The air of an October morning fluttered the lace at their breasts and lifted the long brown hair of the younger man from his shoulders. His companion was tall, alert, bronzed, grey-headed, with an eagle eye and a glance of authority. He laid his hand on the shoulder of the younger man and said: "I am glad you have come, Iberville, for I need you, as I need all your brave family--I could spare not one."

"You honour me, sir," was the reply; "and, believe me, there is none in Quebec but thanks God that their governor is here before Phips rounds Isle Orleans yonder."

"You did nobly while I was away there in Montreal waiting for the New Yorkers to take it--if they could. They were a sorry rabble, for they rushed on La Prairie, that meagre place,--massacred and turned tail."

"That's strange, sir, for they are brave men, stupid though they be. I have fought them."

"Well, well, as that may be! We will give them chance for bravery. Our forts are strong from the Sault au Matelot round to Champigny's palace, the trenches and embankments are well ended, and if they give me but two days more I will hold the place against twice their thirty-four sail and twenty-five hundred men."

"For how long, your excellency?"

Count Frontenac nodded. "Spoken like a soldier. There's the vital point. By the mass, just so long as food lasts! But here we are with near two thousand men, and all the people from the villages, besides Callieres's seven or eight hundred, should they arrive in time--and, pray God they may, for there will be work to do. If they come at us in front here and behind from the Saint Charles, shielding their men as they cross the river, we shall have none too many; but we must hold it."

The governor drew himself up proudly. He had sniffed the air of battle for over fifty years with all manner of enemies, and his heart was in the thing. Never had there been in Quebec a more moving sight than when he arrived from Montreal the evening before, and climbed Mountain Street on his way to the chateau. Women and children pressed round him, blessing him; priests, as he passed, lifted hands in benediction; men cheered and cried for joy; in every house there was thanksgiving that the imperious old veteran had come in time.

Prevost the town mayor, Champigny the Intendant, Sainte-Helene, Maricourt, and Longueil, had worked with the skill of soldiers who knew their duty, and it was incredible what had been done since the alarm had come to Prevost that Phips had entered the St. Lawrence and was anchored at Tadousac.

"And how came you to be here, Iberville?" queried the governor pleasantly. "We scarce expected you."

"The promptings of the saints and the happy kindness of King Louis, who will send my ship here after me. I boarded the first merchantman with its nose to the sea, and landed here soon after you left for Montreal."

"So? Good! See you, see you, Iberville: what of the lady Puritan's marriage with the fire-eating Englishman?"

The governor smiled as he spoke, not looking at Iberville. His glance was upon the batteries in lower town. He had inquired carelessly, for he did not think the question serious at this distance of time. Getting no answer, he turned smartly upon Iberville, surprised, and he was struck by the sudden hardness in the sun-browned face and the flashing eyes. Years had deepened the power of face and form.

"Your excellency will remember," he answered, in a low, cold tone, "that I once was counselled to marry the sword."

The governor laid his hand upon Iberville's shoulder. "Pardon me," he said. "I was not wise or kind. But--I warrant the sword will be your best wife in the end."

"I have a favour to ask, your excellency."

"You might ask many, my Iberville. If all gentlemen here, clerics and laymen, asked as few as you, my life would be peaceful. Your services have been great, one way and another. Ask, and I almost promise now.

"'Tis this. Six months ago you had a prisoner here, captured on the New England border. After he was exchanged you found that he had sent a plan of the fortifications to the Government of Massachusetts. He passed in the name of George Escott. Do you remember?"

"Very well indeed."

"Suppose he were taken prisoner again?"

"I should try him."

"And shoot him, if guilty?"

"Or hang him."

"His name was not Escott. It was Gering--Captain George Gering."

The governor looked hard at Iberville for a moment, and a grim smile played upon his lips. "H'm! How do you guess that?"

"From Perrot, who knows him well."

"Why did Perrot not tell me?"

"Perrot and Sainte-Helene had been up at Sault Sainte Marie. They did not arrive until the day he was exchanged, nor did not know till then. There was no grave reason for speaking, and they said nothing."

"And what imports this?"

"I have no doubt that Mr. Gering is with Sir William Phips below at Tadousac. If he is taken let him be at my disposal."

The governor pursed his lips, then flashed a deep, inquiring glance at his companion. "The new mistress turned against the old, Iberville!" he said. "Gering is her husband, eh? Well, I will trust you: it shall be as you wish--a matter for us two alone."

At that moment Sainte-Helene and Maricourt appeared and presently, in the waning light, they all went down towards the convent of the Ursulines, and made their way round the rock, past the three gates to the palace of the Intendant, and so on to the St. Charles River.

Next morning word was brought that Phips was coming steadily up, and would probably arrive that day. All was bustle in the town, and prayers and work went on without ceasing. Late in the afternoon the watchers from the rock of Quebec saw the ships of the New England fleet slowly rounding the point of the Island of Orleans.

To the eyes of Sir William Phips and his men the great fortress, crowned with walls, towers, and guns, rising three hundred feet above the water, the white banner flaunting from the chateau and the citadel, the batteries, the sentinels upon the walls--were suggestive of stern work. Presently there drew away from Phips's fleet a boat carrying a subaltern with a flag of truce, who was taken blindfold to the Chateau St. Louis. Frontenac's final words to the youth were these: "Bid your master do his best, and I will do mine."

Disguised as a river-man, Iberville himself, with others, rowed the subaltern back almost to the side of the admiral's ship, for by the freak of some peasants the boat which had brought him had been set adrift. As they rowed from the ship back towards the shore, Iberville, looking up, saw, standing on the deck, Phips and George Gering. He had come for this. He stood up in his boat and took off his cap. His long clustering curls fell loose on his shoulders, and he waved a hand with a nonchalant courtesy. Gering sprang forward. "Iberville!" he cried, and drew his pistol.

Iberville saw the motion, but did not stir. He called up, however, in a clear, distinct voice: "Breaker of parole, keep your truce!"

"He is right," said Gering quietly; "quite right." Gering was now hot for instant landing and attack. Had Phips acted upon his advice the record of the next few days might have been reversed. But the disease of counsel, deliberation, and prayer had entered into the soul of the sailor and treasure-hunter, now Sir William Phips, governor of Massachusetts. He delayed too long: the tide turned; there could be no landing that night.

Just after sundown there was a great noise, and the ringing of bells and sound of singing came over the water to the idle fleet.

"What does it mean?" asked Phips of a French prisoner captured at Tadousac.

"Ma foi! That you lose the game," was the reply. "Callieres, the governor of Montreal, with his Canadians, and Nicholas Perrot with his coureurs du bois have arrived. You have too much delay, monsieur."

In Quebec, when this contingent arrived, the people went wild. And Perrot was never prouder than when, in Mountain Street, Iberville, after three years' absence, threw his arms round him and kissed him on each cheek.

It was in the dark hour before daybreak that Iberville and Perrot met for their first talk after the long separation. What had occurred on the day of Jessica's marriage Perrot had, with the Abbe de Casson's help, written to Iberville. But they had had no words together. Now, in a room of the citadel which looked out on the darkness of the river and the deeper gloom of the Levis shore, they sat and talked, a single candle burning, their weapons laid on the table between them.

They said little at first, but sat in the window looking down on the town and the river. At last Iberville spoke. "Tell me it all as you remember it, Perrot." Perrot, usually swift of speech when once started, was very slow now. He felt the weight of every word, and he had rather have told of the scalping of a hundred men than of his last meeting with Jessica. When he had finished, Iberville said: "She kept the letter, you say?"

Perrot nodded, and drew the ring from a pouch which he carried. "I have kept it safe," he said, and held it out. Iberville took it and turned it over in his hand, with an enigmatical smile. "I will hand it to her myself," he said, half beneath his breath.

"You do not give her up, monsieur?"

Iberville laughed. Then he leaned forward, and found Perrot's eyes in the half darkness. "Perrot, she kept the letter, she would have kept the ring if she could. Listen: Monsieur Gering has held to his word; he has come to seek me this time. He knows that while I live the woman is not his, though she bears his name. She married him--Why? It is no matter --he was there, I was not. There were her father, her friends! I was a Frenchman, a Catholic--a thousand things! And a woman will yield her hand while her heart remains in her own keeping. Well, he has come. Now, one way or another, he must be mine. We have great accounts to settle, and I want it done between him and me. If he remains in the ship we must board it. With our one little craft there in the St. Charles we will sail out, grapple the admiral's ship, and play a great game: one against thirty-four. It has been done before. Capture the admiral's ship and we can play the devil with the rest of them. If not, we can die. Or, if Gering lands and fights, he also must be ours.Sainte-Helene and Maricourt know him, and they with myself, Clermont, and Saint Denis, are to lead and resist attacks by land--Frontenac has promised that: so he must be ours one way or another. He must be captured, tried as a spy, and then he is mine--is mine!"

"Tried as a spy--ah, I see! You would disgrace? Well, but even then he is not yours."

Iberville got to his feet. "Don't try to think it out, Perrot. It will come to you in good time. I can trust you--you are with me in all?"

"Have I ever failed you?"

"Never. You will not hesitate to go against the admiral's ship? Think, what an adventure! Remember Adam Dollard and the Long Sault!"

What man in Canada did not remember that handful of men, going out with an antique courage to hold back the Iroquois, and save the colony, and die? Perrot grasped Iberville's hand, and said: "Where you go, I go. Where I go, my men will follow."

Their pact was made. They sat there in silence till the grey light of morning crept slowly in. Still they did not lie down to rest; they were waiting for De Casson. He came before a ray of sunshine had pierced the leaden light.

Tall, massive, proudly built, his white hair a rim about his forehead, his deep eyes watchful and piercing, he looked a soldier in disguise, as indeed he was to-day as much a soldier as when he fought under Turenne forty years before.

The three comrades were together again.

Iberville told his plans. The abbe lifted his fingers in admonition once or twice, but his eyes flashed as Iberville spoke of an attempt to capture the admiral on his own ship. When Iberville had finished, he said in a low voice:

"Pierre, must it still be so--that the woman shall prompt you to these things?"

"I have spoken of no woman, abbe."

"Yet you have spoken." He sighed and raised his hand. "The man--the men--down there would destroy our country. They are our enemies, and we do well to slay. But remember, Pierre--'What God hath joined let no man put asunder!' To fight him as an enemy of your country--well; to fight him that you may put asunder is not well."

A look, half-pained, half-amused, crossed Iberville's face.

"And yet heretics--heretics, abbe"

"Marriage is no heresy."

"H'm-they say different at Versailles."

"Since De Montespan went, and De Maintenon rules?"

Iberville laughed. "Well, well, perhaps not."

They sat silent for a time, but presently Iberville rose, went to a cupboard, drew forth some wine and meat, and put the coffee on the fire. Then, with a gesture as of remembrance, he went to a box, drew forth his own violin, and placed it in the priest's hands. It seemed strange that, in the midst of such great events, the loss or keeping of an empire, these men should thus devote the few hours granted them for sleep; but they did according to their natures. The priest took the instrument and tuned it softly. Iberville blew out the candle. There was only the light of the fire, with the gleam of the slow-coming dawn. Once again, even as years before in the little house at Montreal, De Casson played--now with a martial air. At last he struck the chords of a song which had been a favourite with the Carignan-Salieres regiment.

Instantly Iberville and Perrot responded, and there rang out from three strong throats the words:

> "There was a king of Normandy,
> And he rode forth to war,
> Gai faluron falurette!
> He had five hundred men-no more!
> Gai faluron donde!
>
> "There was a king of Normandy,
> Came back from war again;
> He brought a maid, O, fair was she!
> And twice five hundred men--
> Gai faluron falurette!
> Gai faluron donde!"

They were still singing when soldiers came by the window in the first warm light of sunrise. These caught it up, singing it as they marched on. It was taken up again by other companies, and by the time Iberville presented himself to Count Frontenac, not long after, there was hardly a citizen, soldier, or woodsman, but was singing it.

The weather and water were blustering all that day, and Phips did not move, save for a small attempt--repulsed--by a handful of men to examine the landing. The next morning, however, the attack began. Twelve hundred men were landed at Beauport, in the mud and low water, under one Major Walley. With him was Gering, keen for action--he had per-suaded Phips to allow him to fight on land.

To meet the English, Iberville, Sainte-Helene, and Perrot issued forth with three hundred sharpshooters and a band of Huron Indians. In the skirmish that followed, Iberville and Perrot pressed with a handful of men forward very close to the ranks of the English. In the charge which the New Englander ordered, Iberville and Perrot saw Gering, and they tried hard to reach him. But the movement between made it impossible without running too great risk. For hours the fierce skirmishing went on, but in the evening the French withdrew and the New Englanders made their way towards the St. Charles, where vessels were to meet them, and protect them as they crossed the river and attacked the town in the rear --help that never came. For Phips, impatient, spent his day in a terrible cannonading, which did no great damage to the town--or the cliff. It was a game of thunder, nothing worse, and Walley and Gering with their men were neglected.

The fight with the ships began again at daybreak. Iberville, seeing that Walley would not attack, joined Sainte-Helene and Maricourt at the battery, and one of Iberville's shots brought down the admiral's flagstaff, with its cross of St. George. It drifted towards the shore, and Maurice Joval went out in a canoe under a galling fire and brought it up to Fronte-nac.

Iberville and Sainte-Helene concentrated themselves on the Six Friends-- the admiral's ship. In vain Phips's gunners tried to dislodge them and their guns. They sent ball after ball into her hull and through her rigging; they tore away her mainmast, shattered her mizzenmast, and handled her as viciously as only expert gunners could. The New Englander replied bravely, but Quebec was not destined to be taken by bombardment, and Iberville saw the Six Friends drift, a shattered remnant, out of his line of fire.

It was the beginning of the end. One by one the thirty-four craft drew away, and Walley and Gering were left with their men, unaided in the siege. There was one moment when the cannonading was greatest and the skirmishers seemed withdrawn, that Gering, furious with the delay, almost prevailed upon the cautious Walley to dash across the river and make a desperate charge up the hill, and in at the back door of the town. But Walley was, after all, a merchant and not a soldier, and would not do it. Gering fretted on his chain, sure that Iberville was with the guns against the ships, and would return to harass his New Englanders soon. That evening it turned bitter cold, and without the ammunition promised by Phips, with little or no food and useless field-pieces, their lot was hard.

But Gering had his way the next morning. Walley set out to the Six Friends to represent his case to the admiral. Gering saw how the men chafed, and he sounded a few of them. Their wills were with him they had come to fight, and fight they would, if they could but get the chance. With a miraculous swiftness the whispered word went through the lines. Gering could not command them to it, but if the men went forward he must go with them. The ships in front were silent. Quebec was now interested in these men near the St. Charles River.

As Iberville stood with Frontenac near the palace of the Intendant, watching, he saw the enemy suddenly hurry forward. In an instant he was dashing down to join his brothers, Sainte-Helene, Longueil, and Perrot; and at the head of a body of men they pushed on to get over the ford and hold it, while Frontenac, leading three battalions of troops, got away more slowly. There were but a few hundred men with Iberville, arrayed against Gering's many hundreds; but the French were bush-fighters and the New Englanders were only stout sailors and ploughmen. Yet Gering had no reason to be ashamed of his men that day; they charged bravely, but their enemies were hid to deadly advantage behind trees and thickets, the best sharpshooters of the province.

Perrot had had his orders from Iberville: Iberville himself was, if possible, to engage Gering in a hand-to-hand fight; Perrot, on the other hand, was to cut Gering off from his men and bring him in a prisoner. More than once both had Gering within range of their muskets, but they held their hands, nor indeed did Gering himself, who once also had a chance of bringing Iberville down, act on his opportunity. Gering's men were badly exposed, and he sent them hard at the thickets, clearing the outposts at some heavy loss. His men were now scattered, and he shifted his position so as to bring him nearer the spot where Sainte-Helene and Longueil were pushing forward fresh outposts. He saw the activity of the two brothers, but did not recognise them, and sent a handful of men to dislodge them. Both Sainte-Helene and Longueil exposed themselves for a moment, as they made for an advantageous thicket. Gering saw his opportunity, took a musket from a soldier, and fired. Sainte-Helene fell mortally wounded. Longueil sprang forward with a cry of rage, but a spent ball struck him.

Iberville, at a distance, saw the affair. With a smothered oath he snatched a musket from Maurice Joval, took steady aim and fired. The distance was too great, the wind too strong; he only carried away an epaulet. But

Perrot, who was not far from the fallen brothers, suddenly made a dash within easy range of the rifles of the British, and cut Gering and two of his companions off from the main body. It was done so suddenly that Gering found himself between two fires. His companions drew close to him, prepared to sell their lives dearly, but Perrot called to them to surrender. Gering saw the fruitlessness of resistance and, to save his companions' lives, yielded.

The siege of Quebec was over. The British contented themselves with holding their position till Walley returned bearing the admiral's orders to embark again for the fleet. And so in due time they did--in rain, cold, and gloom.

In a few days Sir William Phips, having patched up his shattered ships, sailed away, with the knowledge that the capture of Quebec was not so easy as finding a lost treasure. He had tried in vain to effect Gering's release.

When Gering surrendered, Perrot took his sword with a grim coolness and said: "Come, monsieur, and see what you think your stay with us may be like."

In a moment he was stopped beside the dead body of Sainte-Helene. "Your musket did this," said Perrot, pointing down. "Do you know him?"

Gering stooped over and looked. "My God-Sainte-Helene!" he cried.

Perrot crossed himself and mumbled a prayer. Then he took from his bosom a scarf and drew it over the face of the dead man. He turned to Longueil.

"And here, monsieur, is another brother of Monsieur Iberville," he said.

Longueil was insensible but not dangerously wounded. Perrot gave a signal and the two brothers were lifted and carried down towards the ford, followed by Perrot and Gering. On their way they met Iberville.

All the brother, the comrade, in Iberville spoke first. He felt Longueil's hand and touched his pulse, then turned, as though he had not seen Gering, to the dead body of Sainte-Helene. Motioning to the men to put it down, he stooped and took Perrot's scarf from the dead face. It was yet warm, and the handsome features wore a smile. Iberville looked for a moment with a strange, cold quietness. He laid his hand upon the brow, touched the cheek, gave a great sigh, and made the sacred gesture over the body; then taking his own handkerchief he spread it over the face. Presently he motioned for the bodies to be carried on.

Perrot whispered to him, and now he turned and look at Gering with a malignant steadiness.

"You have had the great honour, sir," he said, "to kill one of the bravest gentlemen of France. More than once to-day myself and my friend here"--pointing to Perrot "could have killed you. Why did we not? Think you, that you might kill my brother, whose shoe-latchet were too high for you? Monsieur, the sum mounts up." His voice was full of bitterness and hatred. "Why did we spare you?" he repeated, and paused.

Gering could understand Iberville's quiet, vicious anger. He would rather have lost a hand than have killed Sainte-Helene, who had, on board the Maid of Provence, treated him with great courtesy. He only shook his head now.

"Well, I will tell you," said Iberville. "We have spared you to try you for a spy. And after--after! His laugh was not pleasant to hear.

"A spy? It is false!" cried Gering.

"You will remember--monsieur, that once before you gave me the lie!"

Gering made a proud gesture of defiance, but answered nothing. That night he was lodged in the citadel.

A TRAP IS SET

GERING was tried before Governor Frontenac and the full council. It was certain that he, while a prisoner at Quebec, had sent to Boston plans of the town, the condition of the defences, the stores, the general armament and the approaches, for the letter was intercepted.

Gering's defence was straightforward. He held that he had sent the letter at a time when he was a prisoner simply, which was justifiable; not when a prisoner on parole, which was shameless. The temper of the court was against him. Most important was the enmity of the Jesuits, whose hatred of Puritanism cried out for sacrifice. They had seen the work of the saints in every turn of the late siege, and they believed that the Lord had delivered the man into their hands. In secret ways their influence was strong upon many of the council, particularly those who were not soldiers. A soldier can appreciate bravery, and Gering had been courageous. But he had killed one of the most beloved of Canadian officers, the gallant Sainte-Helene! Frontenac, who foresaw an end of which the council could not know, summed up, not unfairly, against Gering.

Gering's defence was able, proud, and sometimes passionate. Once or twice his words stung his judges like whips across their faces. He showed no fear; he asked no mercy. He held that he was a prisoner of war, and entitled to be treated as such. So strong, indeed, was his pleading, so well did his stout courage stand by him, that had Count Frontenac balanced in his favour he might have been quit of the charge of spying. But before the trial Iberville had had solitary talk with Frontenac, in which a request was repeated and a promise renewed.

Gering was condemned to die. It was perhaps the bravest moment of a brave life.

"Gentlemen," he said, "I have heard your sentence, but, careless of military honour as you are, you will not dare put me to death. Do not think because we have failed this once that we shall not succeed again. I tell you, that if, instead of raw Boston sailors, ploughmen and merchant captains, and fishing craft and trading vessels, I had three English war-ships and one thousand men, I would level your town from the citadel to the altar of St. Joseph's. I do not fear to die, nor that I shall die by your will. But, if so, 'twill be with English loathing of injustice."

His speech was little like to mollify his judges, and at his reference to St. Joseph's a red spot showed upon many cheeks, while to the charge against their military honour, Frontenac's eyes lighted ominously. But the governor merely said: "You have a raw temper, sir. We will chasten you with bread and water; and it were well for you, even by your strange religion, to qualify for passage from this world."

Gering was taken back to prison. As he travelled the streets he needed all his fortitude, for his fiery speech had gone abroad, distorted from its meaning, and the common folk railed at him. As chastening, it was good exercise; but when now and again the name of Sainte-Helene rang towards him, a cloud passed over his face; that touched him in a tender corner.

He had not met Iberville since his capture, but now, on entering the prison, he saw his enemy not a dozen paces from the door, pale and stern. Neither made a sign, but with a bitter sigh Gering entered. It was curious how their fortunes had see-sawed, the one against the other, for twelve years.

Left alone in his cell with his straw and bread and water, he looked round mechanically. It was yet after noon. All at once it came to him that this was not the cell which he had left that day. He got up and began to examine it. Like every healthy prisoner, he thought upon means and chances of escape.

It did not seem a regular cell for prisoners, for there was a second door. This was in one corner and very narrow, the walls not coming to a right angle, but having another little strip of wall between. He tried to settle its position by tracing in his mind the way he had come through the prison. Iberville or Perrot could have done so instinctively, but he was not woodsman enough. He thought, however, that the doorway led to a staircase, like most doors of the kind in old buildings. There was the window. It was small and high up from the floor, and even could he loosen the bars, it were not possible to squeeze through. Besides, there was the yard to cross and the outer wall to scale. And that achieved, with the town still full of armed men, he would have a perilous run. He tried the door: it was stoutly fastened; the bolts were on the other side; the key-hole was filled. Here was sufficient exasperation. He had secreted a small knife on his person, and he now sat down, turned it over in his hand, looked up at the window and the smooth wall below it, at the mocking door, then smiled at his own poor condition and gave himself to cheerless meditation.

He was concerned most for his wife. It was not in him to give up till the inevitable was on him and he could not yet believe that Count Frontenac would carry out the sentence. At the sudden thought of the rope--so ignominious, so hateful--he shuddered. But the shame of it was for his wife, who had dissipated a certain selfish and envious strain in him. Jessica had drawn from him the Puritanism which had made him self-conscious, envious, insular.

AN UNTOWARD MESSENGER

A few days after this, Jessica, at her home in Boston,--in the room where she had promised her father to be George Gering's wife,--sat watching the sea. Its slow swinging music came up to her through the October air. Not far from her sat an old man, his hands clasping a chair-arm, a book in his lap, his chin sunk on his breast. The figure, drooping helplessly, had still a distinguished look, an air of honourable pride. Presently he raised his head, his drowsy eyes lighted as they rested on her, and he said: "The fleet has not returned, my dear? Quebec is not yet taken?"

"No, father," she replied, "not yet."

"Phips is a great man--a great man!" he said, chuckling. "Ah, the treasure!"

Jessica did not reply. Her fingers went up to her eyes; they seemed to cool the hot lids.

"Ay, ay, it was good," he added, in a quavering voice, "and I gave you your dowry!"

Now there was a gentle, soft laugh of delight and pride, and he reached out a hand towards her. She responded with a little laugh which was not unlike his, but there was something more: that old sweet sprightliness of her youth, shot through with a haunting modulation,--almost pensiveness, but her face was self-possessed. She drew near, pressed the old man's hand, and spoke softly. Presently she saw that he was asleep.

She sat for some time, not stirring. At last she was about to rise and take him to his room, but hearing noises in the street she stepped to the window. There were men below, and this made her apprehensive. She hurried over, kissed the old man, passed from the room, and met her old servant Hulm in the passage, who stretched out her hand in distress.

"What is it, Hulm?" she asked, a chill at her heart. "Oh, how can I tell you!" was the answer. "Our fleet was beaten, and--and my master is a prisoner."

The wife saw that this was not all. "Tell me everything, Hulm," she said trembling, yet ready for the worst.

"Oh, my dear, dear mistress, I cannot!"

"Hulm, you see that I am calm," she answered. "You are only paining me."

"They are to try him for his life!" She caught her mistress by the waist, but Jessica recovered instantly. She was very quiet, very pale, yet the plumbless grief of her eyes brought tears to Hulm's face. She stood for a moment in deep thought.

"Is your brother Aaron in Boston, Hulm?" she asked presently.

"He is below, dear mistress."

"Ask him to step to the dining-room. And that done, please go to my father. And, Hulm, dear creature, you can aid me better if you do not weep."

She then passed down a side staircase and entered the dining-room. A moment afterwards Aaron Hulm came in.

"Aaron," she said, as he stood confused before her misery, "know you the way to Quebec?"

"Indeed, madame, very well. Madame, I am sorry--"

"Let us not dwell upon it, Aaron. Can you get a few men together to go there?"

"Within an hour."

"Very well, I shall be ready."

"You, madame--ready? You do not think of going?"

"Yes, I am going."

"But, madame, it is not safe. The Abenaquis and Iroquois are not friendly, and--"

"Is this friendly? Is it like a good friend, Aaron Hulm? Did I not nurse your mother when--"

He dropped on one knee, took her hand and kissed it. "Madame," he said loyally, "I will do anything you ask; I feared only for your safety."

An hour afterwards she came into the room where her father still slept. Stooping, she kissed his forehead, and fondled his thin grey hair. Then she spoke to Hulm.

"Tell him," she said, "that I will come back soon: that my husband needs me, and that I have gone to him. Tell him that we will both come back-- both, Hulm, you understand!"

"Dear mistress, I understand." But the poor soul made a gesture of despair.

"It is even as I say. We will both come back," was the quiet reply. "Something as truthful as God Himself tells me so. Take care of my dear father--I know you will; keep from him the bad news, and comfort him."

Then with an affectionate farewell she went to her room, knelt down and prayed. When she rose she said to herself: "I am thankful now that I have no child."

In ten minutes a little company of people, led by Aaron Hulm, started away from Boston, making for a block-house fifteen miles distant, where they were to sleep.

The journey was perilous, and more than once it seemed as if they could not reach Quebec alive, but no member of the party was more cheerful than Jessica. Her bravery and spirit never faltered before the others, though sometimes at night, when lying awake, she had a wild wish to cry out or to end her troubles in the fast-flowing Richelieu. But this was only at night. In the daytime action eased the strain, and at last she was rewarded by seeing from the point of Levis, the citadel of Quebec.

They were questioned and kept in check for a time, but at length Aaron and herself were let cross the river. It was her first sight of Quebec, and its massive, impregnable form struck a chill to her heart: it suggested great sternness behind it. They were passed on unmolested towards the Chateau St. Louis. The anxious wife wished to see Count Frontenac himself and then to find Iberville. Enemy of her country though he was, she would appeal to him. As she climbed the steep steps of Mountain Street, worn with hard travel, she turned faint. But the eyes of curious folk were on her, and she drew herself up bravely.

She was admitted almost at once to the governor. He was at dinner when she came. When her message was brought to him, his brows twitched with surprise and perplexity. He called Maurice Joval, and ordered that she be shown to his study and tendered every courtesy. A few moments later he entered the room. Wonder and admiration crossed his face. He had not thought to see so beautiful a woman. Himself an old courtier, he knew women, and he could understand how Iberville had been fascinated. She had arranged her toilette at Levis, and there were few traces of the long, hard journey, save that her hands and face were tanned. The eloquence of her eyes, the sorrowful, distant smile which now was natural to her, worked upon the old soldier before she spoke a word. And after she had spoken, had pleaded her husband's cause, and appealed to the nobleman's chivalry, Frontenac was moved. But his face was troubled. He drew out his watch and studied it.

Presently he went to the door and called Maurice Joval. There was whispering, and then the young man went away.

"Madame, you have spoken of Monsieur Iberville," said the governor. "Years ago he spoke to me of you."

Her eyes dropped, and then they raised steadily, clearly. "I am sure, sir," she said, "that Monsieur Iberville would tell you that my husband could never be dishonourable. They have been enemies, but noble enemies."

"Yet, Monsieur Iberville might be prejudiced," rejoined the governor. "A brother's life has weight."

"A brother's life!" she broke in fearfully. "Madame, your husband killed Iberville's brother."

She swayed. The governor's arm was as quick to her waist as a gallant's of twenty-five: not his to resist the despair of so noble a creature. He was sorry for her; but he knew that if all had gone as had been planned by Iberville, within a half-hour this woman would be a widow.

With some women, perhaps, he would not have hesitated: he would have argued that the prize was to the victor, and that, Gering gone, Jessica would amiably drift upon Iberville. But it came to him that she was not as many other women. He looked at his watch again, and she mistook the action.

"Oh, your excellency," she said, "do not grudge these moments to one pleading for a life-for justice."

"You mistake, madame," he said; "I was not grudging the time--for myself."

At that moment Maurice Joval entered and whispered to the governor. Frontenac rose.

"Madame," he said, "your husband has escaped." A cry broke from her. "Escaped! escaped!"

She saw a strange look in the governor's eyes.

"But you have not told me all," she urged; "there is more. Oh, your excellency, speak!"

"Only this, madame: he may be retaken and--"

"And then? What then?" she cried.

"Upon what happens then," he as drily as regretfully added, "I shall have no power."

But to the quick searching prayer, the proud eloquence of the woman, the governor, bound though he was to secresy, could not be adamant.

"There is but one thing I can do for you," he said at last. "You know Father Dollier de Casson?"

To her assent, he added: "Then go to him. Ask no questions. If anything can be done, he may do it for you; that he will I do not know."

She could not solve the riddle, but she must work it out. There was the one great fact: her husband had escaped.

"You will do all you can do, your excellency?" she said.

"Indeed, madame, I have done all I can," he said. With impulse she caught his hand and kissed it. A minute afterwards she was gone with Maurice Joval, who had orders to bring her to the abbe's house--that, and no more.

The governor, left alone, looked at the hand that she had kissed and said: "Well, well, I am but a fool still. Yet--a woman in a million!" He took out his watch. "Too late," he added. "Poor lady!"

A few minutes afterwards Jessica met the abbe on his own doorstep. Maurice Joval disappeared, and the priest and the woman were alone together. She told him what had just happened.

"There is some mystery," she said, pain in her voice. "Tell me, has my husband been retaken?"

"Madame, he has."

"Is he in danger?"

The priest hesitated, then presently inclined his head in assent.

"Once before I talked with you," she said, "and you spoke good things. You are a priest of God. I know that you can help me, or Count Frontenac would not have sent me to you. Oh, will you take me to my husband?"

If Count Frontenac had had a struggle, here was a greater. First, the man was a priest in the days when the Huguenots were scattering to the four ends of the earth. The woman and her husband were heretics, and what better were they than thousands of others? Then, Sainte-Helene had been the soldier-priest's pupil. Last of all, there was Iberville, over whom this woman had cast a charm perilous to his soul's salvation. He loved Iberville as his own son. The priest in him decided against the woman; the soldier in him was with Iberville in this event--for a soldier's revenge was its mainspring. But beneath all was a kindly soul which intolerance could not warp, and this at last responded.

His first words gave her a touch of hope. "Madame," he said, "I know not that aught can be done, but come."

FROM TIGER'S CLAW TO LION'S MOUTH

EVERY nation has its traitors, and there was an English renegade soldier at Quebec. At Iberville's suggestion he was made one of the guards of the prison. It was he that, pretending to let Gering win his confidence, at last aided him to escape through the narrow corner-door of his cell.

Gering got free of the citadel--miraculously, as he thought; and, striking off from the road, began to make his way by a roundabout to the St. Charles River, where at some lonely spot he might find a boat. No alarm had been given, and as time passed his chances seemed growing, when suddenly there sprang from the grass round him armed men, who closed in, and at the points of swords and rapiers seized him. Scarcely a word was spoken by his captors, and he did not know who they were, until, after a long detour, he was brought inside a manor-house, and there, in the light of flaring candles, faced Perrot and Iberville. It was Perrot who had seized him.

"Monsieur," said Perrot, saluting, "be sure this is a closer prison than that on the heights." This said, he wheeled and left the room.

The two gentlemen were left alone. Gering folded his arms and stood defiant.

"Monsieur," said Iberville, in a low voice, "we are fortunate to meet so at last."

"I do not understand you," was the reply.

"Then let me speak of that which was unfortunate. Once you called me a fool and a liar. We fought and were interrupted. We met again, with the same ending, and I was wounded by the man Bucklaw. Before the wound was healed I had to leave for Quebec. Years passed, you know well how. We met in the Spaniards' country, where you killed my servant; and again at Fort Rupert, you remember. At the fort you surrendered before we had a chance to fight. Again, we were on the hunt for treasure. You got it; and almost in your own harbour I found you, and fought you and a greater ship with you, and ran you down. As your ship sank you sprang from it to my own ship--a splendid leap. Then you were my guest, and we could not fight; all--all unfortunate."

He paused. Gering was cool; he saw Iberville's purpose, and he was ready to respond to it.

"And then?" asked Gering. "Your charge is long--is it finished?"

A hard light came into Iberville's eyes.

"And then, monsieur, you did me the honour to come to my own country. We did not meet in the fighting, and you killed my brother." Iberville crossed himself. "Then"--his voice was hard and bitter--"you were captured; no longer a prisoner of war, but one who had broken his parole. You were thrown into prison, were tried and condemned to death. There remained two things: that you should be left to hang, or an escape--that we should meet here and now."

"You chose the better way, monsieur."

"I treat you with consideration, I hope, monsieur." Gering waved his hand in acknowledgment, and said: "What weapons do you choose?"

Iberville quietly laid on the table a number of swords. "If I should survive this duel, monsieur," questioned Gering, "shall I be free?"

"Monsieur, escape will be unnecessary."

"Before we engage, let me say that I regret your brother's death."

"Monsieur, I hope to deepen that regret," answered Iberville quietly. Then they took up their swords.

AT THE GATES OF MISFORTUNE

MEANWHILE the abbe and Jessica were making their way swiftly towards the manor-house. They scarcely spoke as they went, but in Jessica's mind was a vague horror. Lights sparkled on the crescent shore of Beauport, and the torches of fishermen flared upon the St. Charles. She looked back once towards the heights of Quebec and saw the fires of many homes--many homes--they scorched her eyes. She asked no questions. The priest beside her was silent, not looking at her at all. Atlast he turned and said:

"Madame, whatever has happened, whatever may happen, I trust you will be brave."

"Monsieur l'Abbe" she answered, "I have travelled from Boston here--can you doubt it?"

The priest sighed. "May the hope that gave you strength remain, ma-dame!"

A little longer and then they stood within a garden thick with plants and trees. As they passed through it, Jessica was vaguely aware of the rich fragrance of fallen leaves and the sound of waves washing the foot of the cliffs.

The abbe gave a low call, and almost instantly Perrot stood before them. Jessica recognised him. With a little cry she stepped to him quickly and placed her hand upon his arm. She did not seem conscious that he was her husband's enemy: her husband's life was in danger, and it must be saved at any cost. "Monsieur," she said, "where is my husband? You know. Tell me."

Perrot put her hand from his arm gently, and looked at the priest in doubt and surprise.

The abbe said not a word, but stood gazing off into the night.

"Will you not tell me of my husband?" she repeated. "He is within that house?" She pointed to the manor-house. "He is in danger, I will go to him."

She made as if to go to the door, but he stepped before her.

"Madame," he said, "you cannot enter."

Just then the moon shot from behind a cloud, and all their faces could be seen. There was a flame in Jessica's eyes which Perrot could not stand, and he turned away. She was too much the woman to plead weakly.

"Tell me," she said, "whose house this is." "Madame, it is Monsieur Iberville's."

She could not check a gasp, but both the priest and the woodsman saw how intrepid was the struggle in her, and they both pitied.

"Now I understand! Oh, now I understand!" she cried. "A plot was laid. He was let escape that he might be cornered here--one single man against a whole country. Oh, cowards, cowards!"

"Pardon me, madame," said Perrot, bristling up, "not cowards. Your husband has a chance for his life. You know Monsieur Iberville--he is a man all honour. More than once he might have had your husband's life, but he gave it to him."

Her foot tapped the ground impatiently, her hands clasped before her. "Go on, oh, go on!" she said. "What is it? why is he here? Have you no pity, no heart?" She turned towards the priest. "You are a man of God. You said once that you would help me make peace between my husband and Monsieur Iberville, but you join here with his enemies."

"Madame, believe me, you are wrong. I have done all I could: I have brought you here."

"Yes, yes; forgive me," she replied. She turned to Perrot again. "It is with you, then. You helped to save my life once--what right have you to destroy it now? You and Monsieur Iberville gave me the world when it were easy to have lost it; now when the world is everything to me because my husband lives in it, you would take his life and break mine."

Suddenly a thought flashed into her mind. Her eyes brightened, her hand trembled towards Perrot, and touched him. "Once I gave you something, monsieur, which I had worn on my own bosom. That little gift--of a grateful girl, tell me, have you it still?"

Perrot drew from his doublet the medallion she had given him, and fingered it uncertainly.

"Then you value it," she added. "You value my gift, and yet when my husband is a prisoner, to what perilous ends God only knows, you deny me to him. I will not plead; I ask as my right; I have come from Count Fronte-nac; he sent me to this good priest here. Were my husband in the citadel now I should be admitted. He is here with the man who, you know, once said he loved me. My husband is wickedly held a prisoner; I ask for entrance to him."

Pleading, apprehension, seemed gone from her; she stood superior to her fear and sorrow. The priest reached a hand persuasively towards Perrot, and he was about to speak, but Perrot, coming close to the troubled wife, said: "The door is locked; they are there alone. I cannot let you in, but come with me. You have a voice--it may be heard. Come."

Presently all three were admitted into the dim hallway.

IN WHICH THE SWORD IS SHEATHED

How had it gone with Iberville and Gering?

THE room was large, scantily, though comfortably, furnished. For a moment after they took up their swords they eyed each other calmly. Iberville presently smiled: he was recalling that night, years ago, when by the light of the old Dutch lantern they had fallen upon each other, swordsmen, even in those days, of more than usual merit. They had practised greatly since. Iberville was the taller of the two, Gering the stouter. Iberville's eye was slow, calculating, penetrating; Gering's was swift, strangely vigilant. Iberville's hand was large, compact, and supple; Gering's small and firm.

They drew and fell on guard. Each at first played warily. They were keen to know how much of skill was likely to enter into this duel, for each meant that it should be deadly. In the true swordsman there is found that curious sixth sense, which is a combination of touch, sight, apprehension, divination. They had scarcely made half a dozen passes before each knew that he was pitted against a master of the art--an art partly lost in an age which better loves the talk of swords than the handling of them. But the advantage was with Iberville, not merely because of more practice,--Gering made up for that by a fine certainty of nerve,--but because he had a prescient quality of mind, joined to the calculation of the perfect gamester.

From the first Iberville played a waiting game. He knew Gering's impulsive nature, and he wished to draw him on, to irritate him, as only one swordsman can irritate another. Gering suddenly led off with a disengage from the carte line into tierce, and, as he expected, met the short parry and riposte. Gering tried by many means to draw Iberville's attack, and, failing to do so, played more rapidly than he ought, which was what Iberville wished.

Presently Iberville's chance came. In the carelessness of annoyance, Gering left part of his sword arm uncovered, while he was meditating a complex attack, and he paid the penalty by getting a sharp prick from Iberville's sword-point. The warning came to Gering in time. When they crossed swords again, Iberville, whether by chance or by momentary want of skill, parried Gering's disengage from tierce to carte on to his own left shoulder.

Both had now got a taste of blood, and there is nothing like that to put the lust of combat into a man. For a moment or two the fight went on with no special feat, but so hearty became the action that Iberville, seeing Gering flag a little,--due somewhat to loss of blood, suddenly opened such a rapid attack on the advance that it was all Gering could do to parry, without thought of riposte, the successive lunges of the swift blade. As he retreated, Gering felt, as he broke ground, that he was nearing the wall, and, even as he parried, incautiously threw a half-glance over his shoulder to see how near. Iberville saw his chance, his finger was shaping a fatal lunge, when there suddenly came from the hallway a woman's voice. So weird was it that both swordsmen drew back, and once more Gering's life was waiting in the hazard.

Strange to say, Iberville recognised the voice first. He was angered with himself now that he had paused upon the lunge and saved Gering. Suddenly there rioted in him the disappointed vengeance of years. He had lost her once by sparing this man's life. Should he lose her again? His sword flashed upward.

At that moment Gering recognised his wife's voice, and he turned pale. "My wife!" he exclaimed.

They closed again. Gering was now as cold as he had before been ardent, and he played with malicious strength and persistency. His nerves seemed of iron. But there had come to Iberville the sardonic joy of one who plays for the final hazard, knowing that he shall win. There was one great move he had reserved for the last. With the woman's voice at the door beseeching, her fingers trembling upon the panel, they could not prolong the fight. Therefore, at the moment when Gering was pressing Iberville hard, the Frenchman suddenly, with a trick of the Italian school, threw his left leg en arriere and made a lunge, which ordinarily would have spitted his enemy, but at the critical moment one word came ringing clearly through the locked door. It was his own name, not Iberville, but--"Pierre! Pierre!"

He had never heard the voice speak that name. It put out his judgment, and instead of his sword passing through Gering's body it only grazed his ribs.

Perhaps there was in him some ancient touch of superstition, some sense of fatalism, which now made him rise to his feet and throw his sword upon the table.

"Monsieur," he said cynically, "again we are unfortunate."

Then he went to the door, unlocked it, and threw it open upon Jessica. She came in upon them trembling, pale, yet glowing with her anxiety.

Instantly Iberville was all courtesy. One could not have guessed that he had just been engaged in a deadly conflict. As his wife entered, Gering put his sword aside. Iberville closed the door, and the three stood looking at each other for a moment. Jessica did not throw herself into her husband's arms. The position was too painful, too tragic, for even the great emotion in her heart. Behind Iberville's courtesy she read the deadly mischief. But she had a power born for imminent circumstances, and her mind was made up as to her course. It had been made up when, at the critical moment, she had called out Iberville's Christian name. She rightly judged that this had saved her husband's life, for she guessed that Iberville was the better swordsman.

She placed her hands with slight resistance on the arms of her husband, who was about to clasp her to his breast, and said: "I am glad to find you, George." That was all.

He also had heard that cry, "Pierre," and he felt shamed that his life was spared because of it--he knew well why the sword had not gone through his body. She felt less humiliation, because, as it seemed to her, she had a right to ask of Iberville what no other woman could ask for her husband.

A moment after, at Iberville's request, they were all seated. Iberville had pretended not to notice the fingers which had fluttered towards him. As yet nothing had been said about the duel, as if by tacit consent. So far as Jessica was concerned it might never have happened. As for the men, the swords were there, wet with the blood they had drawn, but they made no sign. Iberville put meat and wine and fruit upon the table, and pressed Jessica to take refreshment. She responded, for it was in keeping with her purpose. Presently Iberville said, as he poured a glass of wine for her: "Had you been expected, madame, there were better entertainment."

"Your entertainment, monsieur," she replied, "has two sides,"--she glanced at the swords,--"and this is the better."

"If it pleases you, madame."

"I dare not say," she returned, "that my coming was either pleasant or expected."

He raised his glass towards her: "Madame, I am proud to pledge you once more. I recall the first time that we met."

Her reply was instant. "You came, an ambassador of peace to the governor of New York. Monsieur, I come an ambassador of peace to you."

"Yes, I remember. You asked me then what was the greatest, bravest thing I ever did. You ever had a buoyant spirit, madame."

"Monsieur," she rejoined, with feeling, "will you let me answer that question for you now? The bravest and greatest thing you ever did was to give a woman back her happiness."

"Have I done so?"

"In your heart, yes, I believe. A little while ago my husband's life and freedom were in your hands--you will place them in mine now, will you not?"

Iberville did not reply directly. He twisted his wineglass round, sipped from it pleasantly, and said: "Pardon me, madame, how were you admitted here?"

She told him.

"Singular, singular!" he replied; "I never knew Perrot fail me before. But you have eloquence, madame, and he knew, no doubt, that you would always be welcome to my home."

There was that in his voice which sent the blood stinging through Gering's veins. He half came to his feet, but his wife's warning, pleading glance brought him to his chair again.

"Monsieur, tell me," she said, "will you give my husband his freedom?"

"Madame, his life is the State's."

"But he is in your hands now. Will you not set him free? You know that the charge against him is false--false. He is no spy. Oh, monsieur, you and he have been enemies, but you know that he could not do a dishonourable thing."

"Madame, my charges against him are true."

"I know what they are," she said earnestly, "but this strife is not worthy of you, and it is shaming me. Monsieur, you know I speak truly.

"You called me Pierre a little while ago," he said; "will you not now?"

His voice was deliberate, every word hanging in its utterance. He had a courteous smile, an apparent abandon of manner, but there was devilry behind all, for here, for the first time, he saw this woman, fought for and lost, in his presence with her husband, begging that husband's life of him. Why had she called him Pierre? Was it because she knew it would touch a tender corner of his heart? Should that be so--well, he would wait.

"Will you listen to me?" she asked, in a low gentle voice.

"I love to hear you speak," was his reply, and he looked into her eyes as he had boldly looked years before, but his gaze made hers drop. There was revealed to her all that was in his mind.

"Then, hear me now," she said slowly. "There was a motherless young girl. She had as fresh and cheerful a heart as any in the world. She had not many playmates, but there was one young lad who shared her sports and pleasant hours, who was her good friend. Years passed; she was nearing womanhood, the young man was still her friend, but in his mind there had come something deeper. A young stranger also came, handsome, brave, and brilliant. He was such a man as any girl could like and any man admire. The girl liked him, and she admired him. The two young men quarreled; they fought; and the girl parted them. Again they would have fought, but this time the girl's 'life was in danger. The stranger was wounded in saving her. She owed him a debt--such a debt as only a woman can feel; because a woman loves a noble deed more than she loves her life--a good woman."

She paused, and for an instant something shook in her throat. Her husband looked at her with a deep wonder. And although Iberville's eyes played with his glass of wine, they were fascinated by her face, and his ear was strangely charmed by her voice.

"Will you go on?" he said.

"The three parted. The girl never forgot the stranger. What might have happened if he had always been near her, who can tell--who can tell? Again in later years the two men met, the stranger the aggressor--without due cause."

"Pardon me, madame, the deepest cause," said Iberville meaningly.

She pretended not to understand, and continued: "The girl, believing that what she was expected to do would be best for her, promised her hand in marriage. At this time the stranger came. She saw him but for a day, for an hour, then he passed away. Time went on again, and the two men met in battle--men now, not boys; once more the stranger was the victor. She married the defeated man. Perhaps she did not love him as much as he loved her, but she knew that the other love, the love of the stranger, was impossible--impossible. She came to care for her husband more and more-- she came to love him. She might have loved the stranger--who can tell? But a woman's heart cannot be seized as a ship or a town. Believe me, monsieur, I speak the truth. Years again passed: her husband's life was in the stranger's hand. Through great danger she travelled to plead for her husband's life. Monsieur, she does not plead for an unworthy cause. She pleads for justice, in the name of honourable warfare, for the sake of all good manhood. Will--will you refuse her?"

She paused. Gering's eyes were glistening. Her honesty, fine eloquence, and simple sincerity, showed her to him in a new, strong light. Upon Iberville, the greater of the two, it had a greater effect. He sat still for a moment, looking at the woman with the profound gaze of one moved to the soul. Then he got to his feet slowly, opened the door, and quietly calling Perrot, whispered to him. Perrot threw up his hands in surprise, and hurried away.

Then Iberville shut the door, and came back. Neither man had made any show of caring for their wounds. Still silent, Iberville drew forth linen and laid it upon the table. Then he went to the window, and as he looked through the parted curtains out upon the water--the room hung over the edge of the cliff-he bound his own shoulder. Gering had lost blood, but weak as he was he carried himself well. For full half an hour Iberville stood motionless while the wife bound her husband's wounds.

At length the door opened and Perrot entered. Iberville did not hear him at first, and Perrot came over to him. "All is ready, monsieur," he said.

Iberville, nodding, came to the table where stood the husband and wife, and Perrot left the room. He picked up a sword and laid it beside Gering, then waved his hand towards the door.

"You are free to go, monsieur," he said. "You will have escort to your country. Go now--pray, go quickly."

He feared he might suddenly repent of his action, and going to the door, he held it open for them to pass. Gering picked up the sword, found the belt and sheath, and stepped to the doorway with his wife. Here he paused as if he would speak to Iberville: he was ready now for final peace. But Iberville's eyes looked resolutely away, and Gering sighed and passed into the hallway. Now the wife stood beside Iberville. She looked at him steadily, but at first he would not meet her eye. Presently, however, he did so.

"Good-bye," she said brokenly, "I shall always remember--always."

His reply was bitter. "Good-bye, madame: I shall forget."

She made a sad little gesture and passed on, but presently turned, as if she could not bear that kind of parting, and stretched out her hands to him.

"Monsieur--Pierre!" she cried, in a weak, choking voice.

With hot frank impulse he caught both her hands in his and kissed them. "I shall--remember," he said, with great gentleness.

Then they passed from the hallway, and he was alone. He stood looking at the closed door, but after a moment went to the table, sat down, and threw his head forward in his arms.

An hour afterwards, when Count Frontenac entered upon him, he was still in the same position. Frontenac touched him on the arm, and he rose. The governor did not speak, but caught him by the shoulders with both hands, and held him so for a moment, looking kindly at him. Iberville picked up his sword from the table and said calmly:

"Once, sir, you made it a choice between the woman and the sword."

Then he raised the sword and solemnly pressed his lips against the hilt-cross.